Praise for *A Legend of the Future*

"Finally, we have the chance to read a landmark work from one of Cuba's greatest science fiction writers… You'll want to prepare yourself for *Legend*. It's been compared to Clarke's *2001*, and like that remarkable text, de Rojas's will blow your mind in a good way… Addictive."
—*SF Signal*, 4.5-star review

"The best and most popular novelist of this genre that the Island has ever given us."
—Yoss, author of *A Planet for Rent*

"One of the best science fiction writers in Cuba—and, until his death, one of the best Cuban storytellers alive."
—*Cubaencuentro*

"The most elevated figure in Cuban science fiction."
—*Axxón*

"His work is full of complex extravagance of the imagination, with a thousand and one narrative hooks… In consideration of such versatile, profound, detailed, authentic, excellent work, it's certain that this author—one of the few Cubans alive with the capacity and power to write genuine bestsellers—would have a good place in the Parnassus of the last few decades' greats."
—*Isliada*

"The best science fiction writer in Cuba; the only possible debate is which of his works is the best… His trilogy of *Spiral*, *A Legend of the Future*, and *The Year 200* is still the best of Cuban science fiction."
—*Cuenta Regresiva*

A LEGEND
OF THE FUTURE

Agustín de Rojas

Translated from the Spanish by Nick Caistor

RESTLESS BOOKS
Brooklyn, New York

Ellison, Stavans, and Hochstein LP
232 3rd Street, Suite A111
Brooklyn, NY 11215

publisher@restlessbooks.com
www.restlessbooks.com

To Silvio Rodríguez
Singer of *Homo Sapiens*

Hannah, can you hear me, wherever you are? Look up, Hannah: the clouds are lifting, the sun is breaking through, we are coming out of the darkness into the light, we are coming into a new world, a kindlier world where men will rise above their hate, their greed and brutality... Look up, Hannah, the soul of man has been given wings and at last he is beginning to fly; he is flying into the rainbow, into the light of hope... Look up, Hannah, look up!

—Charlie Chaplin, *The Great Dictator*

A LEGEND
OF THE FUTURE

Prologue

At first, the white-striped green disk grew slowly. Then quickly, very quickly, too quickly. Almost unconsciously, the man falling from the sky held his breath a second before his boots plunged into the tufts of grass, snapping off stems, burying them in the still damp earth.

The airman straightened up, his hand reaching for the black button on his chest. He found it and pressed. Behind him, the monotonous drone of the levitator ceased. The straps tightened on his shoulders. Isanusi listened closely to the silent wind... He surveyed the horizon beyond the low circle of chalky rocks. Hungry for green, he found it in the dark foliage of distant forests, in the light, shiny green of the grass together with other pale, faded colors, and green, green, and more green... His eyes drank in all the color, even that of the mosses and lichens staining the rocks. Isanusi took a long, deep breath of the air filled with the odor of plants, and smiled.

On the bridge of the ship, warning lights were blinking softly. Leaning over the instrument panel, Alix asked,

"What's going on, Palas?"

Gauges spun until the figures became confused, illegible blotches. A hundred multi-colored needles quivered in their glass prisons: right, then left. The monitor panel spoke:

"Damage to protective shield. Energy loss from forward inductor, not controllable."

Alix stroked her chin.

"What do you suggest?"

"Pull back protective shield. Human inspection of the damage area; depending on result, either repair or replace."

"Thanks for..."

Alix was unable to finish the traditional sign-off. The panel interrupted her, its words tumbling out:

"Attention, attention: strict time limit for taking decision, energy imbalance gro..."

Palas' voice faded away. Alix's right hand automatically disconnected the protective magnetic shield. With her left she switched on the intercom. The sharp blast of the alarm echoed throughout the craft.

"Emergency, emergency. Pavel, Kay, prepare to go outside. Rest of the crew, await instructions."

She flicked off the intercom. Her hands returned to the controls, crisscrossing between rheostats and switches, questioning, proposing, arguing. A drop of sweat—the first—slid down her furrowed brow.

At the exact center of the landing zone rose a grey monolith. Standing in front of it, Isanusi finished reading the sign on the plaque, then felt for the top of the stone. He pressed lightly, and a square opening appeared. Plunging his arms into the cool interior, he grasped and removed first one sack, then another, and another. He laid them on the ground, next to the levitator. Gusts of wind rippled through them, while Isanusi slowly undressed. The shadows were shortening, and the sun began to warm his dark skin. Carefully folding his clothes, he placed them inside the stone, and closed it.

"...Just think, that tiny cosmic pebble, barely a kilo in mass, is wandering its leisurely way through space, without the slightest notion that our ship is rushing to meet it, at one hundred and fifty kilometers a second..."

"Shut up, Pavel."

The spacesuited figure in front of Kay turned, revealing the narrow transparent visor and the dark gleam of Pavel's eyes behind it.

"I can shut up, but I can't stop thinking. You ought to be doing the same, and get a move on. Look, you haven't even done up your clasps yet..."

Pavel's gloves moved rapidly and precisely to seal Kay's suit and helmet.

"There. Don't think or say anything, if you like, but don't waste time. Try your suit."

Kay walked clumsily across the airlock. The safety line snaked out behind her, hissing gently... Her gloves brushed the tangle of keys on her chest, then dropped to her sides.

"Ready?"

Her response was a slight nod. Pavel licked his lips and announced, "We're all set to go, Alix."

The air pumps came on. As the air in the hatch was sucked out, the creases in their space suits smoothed. Soon there were just two inflated figures waiting for the outer door to open.

The sun reflected blue glints off the metal. Isanusi carefully ran the tip of his thumb along the sharp blade. His lips parted slightly, revealing strong white teeth. He slipped the knife back into its scabbard. He picked the sack up and slung it over his shoulder, then strode off into the green sea surrounding him. The knife sheath rubbed against his thigh at every step, and the sack swung rhythmically between his shoulder blades. At first, a straight black line appeared. It widened, to reveal the bright glow of a thousand distant stars. Pavel and Kay reduced the transparency of their visors and everything began to look like a clear night sky on Earth. They moved forward, Pavel climbing the vertical ladder. Kay watched him as he moved outside the hull of the ship, his helmet glinting under the impact of the rarefied atoms of interplanetary dust. She followed him, her eyes fixed on Pavel's shimmering left side; the right-hand part of his suit, still in darkness, was almost invisible.

"Pavel, Alix speaking."

"I'm listening."

"I suggest you don't waste time checking the inductor. Better to change it, then you can repair it inside the ship. Do you agree?"

"Yes."

They walked bent over across the gleaming hull, their magnetic boots clacking as they first clung to it and then were released… Up ahead of them, enveloped in a cold halo of light, the prow of the spaceship loomed.

The glassy surface was broken, the stones at the bottom shimmered. Isanusi raised his cupped hands and drank. Streams of water ran down his chest, rushing to return to the river…

They could feel the dull vibration through the soles of their boots. Bending over still further, Pavel and Kay laid their hands on the ship's luminous hull and peered down. From a gash that had not been there a moment earlier, a liquid mass had poured out, turning solid almost immediately. A golden bubble now rose from the smooth surface of the hull. The two suited figures remained still for a long while, without saying a word.

"Attention everyone, attention: the meteorite did not penetrate the inner hull. It was stopped by the densiplasma."

Alix fell silent, and the two of them breathed a sigh of relief. Pavel straightened up and continued his... advance.

"Pavel?"

"Kay?"

"Say something. Anything."

A forced smile inside a helmet.

"You asked for it..."

Isanusi shook his hands. The drops of water splashed onto the spiky leaves of the bushes, the naked earth, his own body. For no apparent reason, he shouted and laughed as he strode into the icy water.

"...We were walking through the park as usual... No! Now I remember, he was only looking at the ground. He didn't look up at the sky once, Kay. And I didn't know what to say to him... We walked along in silence, not looking at each other. Then on our way back, he began to talk. He told me he understood now how absurd it was to be thinking of flights to other planets, when there was still so much to do on our own. That he regretted all the wasted years, and was pleased his group had not been chosen..."

All of a sudden, Alix's voice sounded in their helmets:

"And what did you say to him, Pavel?"

"Nothing. What could I say?"

"You're asking me? When you're the one who 's talking all the time?"

Pavel did not respond. His hands slowed as he groped cautiously towards the damaged cylinder at the nose of their ship. Kay's jaws moved fitfully... she asked sharply,

"Alix, do you realize what you've done?"

"But Kay, Pavel is always..."

"How could you interrupt him? Keep talking, Pavel, I understand you. Alix only said that because she's nervous. She... But carry on, Pavel, I'd like to hear what you have to say."

For what seemed like interminable seconds there were only random sounds and static. Then Pavel's murmuring voice began again.

"Erik and I had been together since precosmic days. I've asked myself a thousand times why they didn't include him and Tania in our group... You're not necessarily to blame for that, Alix. You have to understand, after all these years..."

His movements gradually speeded up. A round rod popped out of the cylinder and fell into Pavel's gloves. Kay took the replacement inductor out of her suit, and passed it to Pavel. He handed her the damaged one, and she stowed it away.

"...something momentary, transitory. As time goes by..."

The new inductor disappeared inside the cylinder. Pavel's agile hands started the sealing procedure.

Singing, with the water frothing around his knees, Isanusi took his time returning to the sun, the heat... His toes were sucked into the mud, then scaled the steep bank, and led him across to the abandoned sack. Isanusi stretched out and waited, eyes closed, for the sun to dry his skin.

... What can it mean?
He, before whom all tremble
Kissing the dry grass, in tears...
Suddenly lifting his hand to proclaim:
From now on I am no longer your king!
Death on one's native shores
Is more beloved than glory in distant lands!

A brief silence...

"Maikov?"

Gema's eyes flicked open, searching for the videophone... Thondup was smiling at her from the screen. With a sigh, she replied,

"Yes, Maikov here."

Thondup looked at her kindly.

"It's not hard to understand you were hoping to see someone else... Are you going to wake him?"

Gema waved her hand dismissively.

"No? As you wish. But you know him; he won't forgive us for letting him miss something like this."

"What could he do if we woke him? Wait, like the rest of us? No, it's not worth it, Thondup... What did you want to see me for?"

The man's smile broadened.

"For work reasons. I wanted to test the reaction of one of the crew to a situation of stress. Thank you, Gema."

And the videophone clicked off.

The mid-day heat woke Isanusi. Scrambling to his feet, he picked the sack up again, slung it across his warm back. Whistling an old song, he set off once more.

Raising her hands to the back of her head, Alix massaged her aching nape. When she leaned forward again over the controls, she saw a warm yellow light glowing. "Inductor repaired, Pavel and Kay must be on their way back. How we'll laugh, remembering this anxious moment... Not so fast, Alix, they're not back inside yet... Kay was right, I shouldn't have interrupted him, but he could have talked about something else... I have no doubt what led that group to fail. Erik himself..." A flash of light on the panel interrupted her thoughts. She brought her face close to the right-hand screen and studied it. She breathed a sigh of relief. "No, nothing in the locator ... That way of his of reacting, denying everything... And Pavel still defends him! He's a real Neanderthal. Audo wasn't mistaken, there are still lots of them around. They even reach the Cosmic Academy ... Yes, they reach it, but luckily they don't get any further... No, it's not luck, it's justice. It's lucky this happened to us here, where the density of matter is low... How much I want to see you, Thondup... If it had happened in the asteroid belt..." She looked at the configuration of the lights on the controls. "No, they're not back inside yet." She checked the time and smiled. "Of course, they couldn't have finished even if they had been running. How slowly time passes! Another hour until I'm relieved... I'd love to see his face when he comes in here. I wonder if they've already woken him up?" Another glance at the panel. "No, not yet... Nothing in the locator. We're fortunate, a bigger meteorite, and... Why worry about something that hasn't happened? Concentrate on what you have to do, Alix… They must be at the hatch by now… As soon as I'm relieved, I'll go straight to see Pavel. I'll tell him exactly what I think of Erik. Pavel is far too gullible, too trusting with everybody…"

Isanusi judged the distance. A run-up, a leap, and he would be on the far side of the ravine. He walked back a dozen paces, flexing his muscles… Then he began to run, looking closely at the rapidly approaching spot from where he needed to launch himself, and the small bush on the far side that he had to reach.

The alarms shrieked. Instinctively, Alix reached for the monitor panel with both hands, trying to take control. To no avail.

He leapt into the air, his supple body straining, his eyes fixed on the small bush zooming towards him. He could make out every one of its leaves with complete clarity as they swayed in the gentle breeze… He could feel his taut muscles as he prepared to hit the ground again. All of a sudden, a thousand suns exploded.

They grew and grew, and then shrank, only to expand once more, scorching his dazzled eyes. The heat washed over him in dense waves, enveloping him, burning every cell in his body. He rolled around, crying out noiselessly. Every muscle, every fiber was on fire, shriveling up, charred.

A saving darkness descended. Everything was suddenly snuffed out, even the pain.

Part One

The falcon fell from the sky with a wounded breast… The snake was alarmed, and slithered out of the way. Staring into the bird's eyes, it hissed:

"Tell me, are you dying?"

—Maxim Gorky, *The Song of the Falcon*

Wednesday December 29, 2038
18:23 hours

"Welcome… Come in and sit down."

Floating among the shadows, Isanusi crossed a vaguely familiar… space? And reached where he had previously been a week? A century? A year ago?

"We have good news for you. Your group has been chosen…"

An age-old thought surfaced: "*To do what?*"… An important task. Really important, Isanusi. You are to test a new kind of interplanetary ship, the *Sviatagor*…"

"A test flight, not an exploration."

For the second time, he felt a stab of disappointment.

"…Your task is a special one. For the first time, you will be exploring at the same time as you are making a test flight."

The memory of a racing pulse.

"*Well then? Where to?*"

"Destination, Saturn. To be precise, one of its satellites: Titan."

"Titan? Yes, Titan ... Titan!"

The Voice waited for Isanusi to digest this, and then spoke again:

"Naturally, much is expected of the research you will carry out on that satellite ... But more, much more, from the simple fact that you travel there, reach the satellite, and *return* ... Let me explain. Until now it has been an unbreakable rule that we should test any new interplanetary spacecraft in conditions as close as possible to their normal tasks, and only subsequently would we send them off on the missions for which they were designed. It's impossible to deny that this method was useful, as long as we were only hopping between the inner planets in our solar system, but now that we are reaching beyond the asteroid belt it is showing severe limitations. We have to work with our eyes on tomorrow, Isanusi, and tomorrow means the stars ... The first projects for manned interstellar spaceships are underway, and to test a ship destined, let's say, for Alpha Centauri, not even a journey to Pluto would be sufficient. We will only know if the designers were right when the ship returns from Alpha ... In this context, any test flight would be nothing more than a huge waste of resources, and we can't afford that luxury. We have to bear in mind that reaching out to the stars isn't mankind's only concern, Isanusi."

The Voice paused, perhaps to recover its breath. Then it went on, in a more practical tone:

"But let's get back to *Sviatagor*. It could of course be tested in another expedition to the satellites of Jupiter. That would mean we spent the equivalent of a half a dozen normal flights to the same destination in the old spaceships. And we need to do those half-dozen flights to supply the bases we have there. That's one of the reasons why *Sviatagor* will head directly to Saturn. The other is the stars; we cannot wait for when that opportunity to break the psychological barrier of 'test first, then explore.' Isanusi, I am sure you are aware that it has not been easy taking this decision to the Cosmic Council; too much is at stake. Some expeditions have failed to return, whether they were test flights or exploratory ones, even though the established rules were strictly followed. Those failures were seen as an inevitable price to be paid because of all the unforeseen factors... But if you do not come back, it will be seen as the inevitable consequence of breaking a completely essential security norm... for which the Council will have to pay. Interstellar travel will also pay: it will be put back decades, possibly centuries. And although it is not mankind's only concern, we must, we need to reach the stars... Do you understand your mission now?"

The unexpectedly loud echo of his own voice resonated inside Isanusi's skull:

"I understand."

A shadow among shadows, the memory of a weary smile.

"I think we can proceed to more practical details. The fundamental ones; you'll have plenty of time to get to know all about *Sviatagor*. However, I must stress its essential difference with earlier models: its speed, which is a real quantitative difference. 144 kilometers per second in gravity-free flight... That's a vital step for long-distance flights. There are limits to lengthening the duration of flights to increase the distance covered. We are already reaching them with the journeys to Jupiter; the relation between time spent at the destination and the time needed to get there and back has become too disproportionate. We have to devote more and more resources to providing for the crews during the voyage, and relatively less for their stay on the planets. Storage facilities are not limitless. The only possible solution was to increase the speed of the spaceship, and that is what we have done with *Sviatagor*.

"But there are serious consequences, Isanusi. The old protective systems will not work. At the new speeds, a collision with even a tiny, almost invisible meteorite would destroy any current vessel. We have developed a system of complementary measures to avoid this happening to *Sviatagor*. Firstly, it has an extraordinarily sensitive radio-detective system, directly linked to the autopilot... which, by the way, is also a novelty; it is the bio-computer Palas, capable of reacting in the nano-seconds needed to avoid a direct collision with meteorites bigger than a decimeter. Even so, that is not sufficient; at that speed, even smaller meteorites could destroy today's spaceships. That is why the *Sviatagor* has a double hull, with a layer of densiplasma between them... I'm sure you know what its properties are?"

Back then, he had been able to nod his head in agreement, but not now. A feeling was growing, merging with his memories of the past: a feeling of fear.

Isanusi wondered, "*Why can't I see? Why can't I move?*"

The disembodied Voice flowed on:

"... At high pressure, conserving its semi-liquid state, and if any meteorite were to pierce the outer hull, it is very likely, almost certain, that the densiplasma would halt it. And no pressure would be lost because of the hole. A small amount of densiplasma would escape, but it would solidify at once, and seal the rupture. And even if the meteorite did penetrate the inner skin, there would be no loss of pressure in the ship, because before it had gone through the inner wall, the outer wall would have closed up again.

"Obviously, it would be better all around if the *Sviatagor* were not hit by any meteorites; even if there were no loss of pressure, they could cause considerable damage. That's why we've introduced a third safety precaution; the spaceship will create around itself a high-intensity magnetic field capable of changing the trajectory of any meteorite enough to avoid a direct hit.

"As you can see, all these safety measures are interrelated and reinforce one another. Also, the crew—that is, you and your companions—will receive the most up-to-date training.

"But I'm straying from my area. Thondup knows much more about that, and can tell you all about the latest developments in suggestocybernetics. Talk to him, and he'll assure you that we have done everything possible, within our power, to make sure you return.

"There's still one small problem we haven't talked about: what to call your group. Since this is a test flight, you ought to be called *Sviatagor*, but as it is also a voyage of exploration, it could also be *Titan*... We think it would be best for you to choose the name you prefer yourselves. Do you agree?"

In the past, Isanusi's reply must have been affirmative.

"Good, then you may withdraw, Isanusi."

Smiling, memory-Isanusi stood up, saying goodbye and withdrawing... Now, real-Isanusi (truly real?) tried to imitate him, but without success. Increasingly concerned, he waited for the Voice to ask him why he wasn't getting up and leaving...

"What could I tell him?"

Summoning all his willpower, Isanusi tried to overcome the paralysis, to move, to see...

He woke up. Without opening his eyes, he let a soothing wave of reassurance flow over him.

"Oh! It was only a nightmare... How nasty!" He shuddered. "But it's over now, forget it, I have to get up." He opened his eyes.

In front of him, all around him, darkness still reigned.

"Have you woken up, Isanusi?"

The air hissed slightly as it left his lungs. It had not been the Voice, as he had feared for a moment.

"Gema; it's Gema."

He could feel his blood racing.

"What if this isn't a nightmare?"

He attempted to express the questions nagging him:

"Why...?" He paused. "What's in my throat?" He tried to swallow non-existent saliva. "I'll find out later." He completed his question:

"Why isn't there any light?"

He could not see Gema's eyes narrowing into slits. He was not aware of her face approaching his or of her hand waving in front of his face. He did not blink.

"The light is on. Don't worry, my love, it must be a side effect of the shock."

"Shock? What shock? What happened to me? And to *Sviatagor*?"

After a short silence, Gema spoke:

"I suppose you must be anxious to hear what happened... I'll try to sum up the little I know. While you were asleep, there was a fault in the magnetic field. Pavel and Kay had to go outside to repair it. While they were, it seems we collided with a meteorite. I lost consciousness. I must have banged into something, I don't remember what. Thondup found me unconscious in the lab and helped me come around. He didn't know what was going on either... We agreed that he would go to the bridge to see how he could help Alix, while I came to wake you up, so that... But the hypnotron was broken, and I saw that... that you weren't well. I brought you to the sick bay less than five minutes ago, and... well, you woke up."

Gema almost smiled, then remembered Isanusi could not see. She went on:

"Now you're my patient. Tell me: can you feel any other unusual physical sensations, apart from the loss of vision?"

Obediently, Isanusi concentrated on his body... His heart was still racing but beating regularly. His lungs were filling and emptying at a normal rhythm. He couldn't feel any pain, either in his head, torso, arms, or legs... But he could feel a strange, unfamiliar sensation:

"It's as if I'm wrapped in cotton wool. But that must be completely subjective; let's see if I can move my muscles."

He tried to lift his arms in front of his face, but nothing happened. Unintentionally, he held his breath. He tried pulling up his legs, but they remained stretched out. "A bad sign." He tried patiently to contract different muscles, testing them one by one. Only his face muscles responded. He relaxed, to regain strength. "It must be something to do with my nervous system." He made a supreme effort of will, struggling to get his unruly body to obey. His face muscles tensed, but that was all.

"Are you in pain?"

He could sense the concern in Gema's voice. Loosening his clenched lips, he whispered:

"No."

"So why is your face so...?"

Isanusi let his face return to normal.

"I can't move, Gema. Only my face; my body won't obey me. It must be another effect of the shock."

"Possibly. I'll have to examine you."

Isanusi waited for the warm touch of Gema's hands. "She's taking a long time."

He asked, "When are you starting?"

Gema raised her head. Her eyes were open wide.

"But I've already... Wait: did you really feel nothing?"

"Nothing."

Her hands moved back inside the pod, gently running over the warm, naked skin:

"Tell me when you feel something."

Time passed. Isanusi moistened his dry lips with his tongue. "It looks like it's really serious." Gritting his teeth, he scolded himself: "That's for Gema to judge, not me." He tried to relax his mind, to empty it of all thoughts. "Just try to feel."

Gema straightened up and shook her head. One lock of hair was still plastered over her left eye; she had to use her hand to lift it from her damp skin. "This could be serious, let's see how far..." She put her hand on Isanusi's shoulder, at first just resting her fingertips on his skin; then pressed as hard as she could.

"Can you still feel nothing?"

It took him some time to reply.

"No, nothing."

Gema removed her hand. For a long while, she stared at the blue imprint of the five half-moons on his dark skin: four of them close together, in a gentle curve; the other set slightly apart, pointing in the opposite direction to the rest. "The deep receptors as well; it is serious. Or possibly... Yes, give him time to recover. But recover from what? You still have to find that out, Gema."

She tried to sound reassuring:

"Very well, my love... For now, the treatment is to get some sleep. Apparently, you need to rest some more."

She searched for a drug to put him to sleep. "There's no doubt it's his nervous system. What he needs is a neurological examination... but the diagnostic machine is out of action. I must tell Pavel or Thondup to fix it... They need to check the hypnotron too; we have to know what it did to Isanusi. That must be the key to all this; if we can't find out what happened there, we're acting in the dark..."

The hand holding the injector shook slightly. "In the dark... poor Isanusi." She jabbed the needle in.

"Now we just wait."

She sat down, only too aware of her dry throat. "This thirst is a nervous reaction, I just drank some water. I have to get a grip…" She listened intently: Isanusi's breathing was deep and regular. "He's asleep…" She stroked the side of the recovery pod, and the clear plastic lid rose and covered it, isolating the sleeping man.

"Hyper-oxygenate him? Or slow down his metabolism?" She shook her head. "I mustn't act if I'm not sure… Better think of something else." She turned her attention away from Isanusi, and the worry at the back of her mind immediately surfaced. "What about the others?"

She turned her head to look at the closed hatch. "Nobody has come… They haven't even tried to communicate with me. Why would that be?" She swiveled her seat to face the videophone, and pressed the buttons one after another. The screen did not light up. "Perhaps the Voice is still transmitting."

She said, "Thondup, Alix… Pavel, Kay… This is Gema, I'm in the sick bay. The visual channel of my intercom is out of action; I don't know if you are receiving me. Tell me if you can hear me, please… If anyone is injured, you can bring them here… Over…"

She held her breath. No sound came from the intercom. "It's broken, and they haven't repaired it yet. They must have more important things to do." She considered the immobile form of Isanusi in the pod. "Yes, I can leave him. Just for a moment, to find out…" She tried to stand up, but everything around her shook, and was lost in a thick mist. Gema dropped back into her seat, waiting for the dizziness to pass.

"There it is again… a little stronger this time, I think. It's only natural; my blood pressure is too high. I haven't had time to recover from the shock yet." She touched her head gingerly. She could feel the pulse beating on the bump beneath her hair. "I ought to go. But in this state I won't be able to… Shall I call on my reserves again? So soon? It's not advisable, but…" She gradually let herself relax, until all the muscles in her body were slack. "Now I can start." She took a deep breath. "One… two… three… four." Her heartbeats grew stronger, more even… "Seven… eight…" The adrenaline started to kick in, dissolving in her rushing bloodstream. "Eleven… Twelve…" She could feel a strange tingling at her fingertips. It spread pleasurably through her limbs, up her now rigid body. "Fifteen…" Her ears dimly perceived the hatch opening. Her overstimulated reflexes brought her back to herself. "Thondup! At last!" She smiled with relief.

"What took you so long?" She paused, and looked with hypertrophied attention at the man advancing towards her. She observed the pronounced limp, the limpness of the hand holding the densiplasma ejector, the exhausted look on his face… "There are more problems," she realized in a panic.

"What about the others? Alix didn't say anything about them returning. Have Pavel and Kay…?"

She could not bring herself to complete the question.

Thondup slumped into the seat next to her. A swollen, bruised knee showed through a tear in his suit. He probed it very gently before replying:

"They didn't have time, Gema. I looked through the porthole in the airlock: it was empty, and the outside hatch was still open…"

"Why didn't you try to bring them in using the safety lines? Perhaps they had just lost consciousness."

"The lines had snapped."

In his mind's eye he saw the thick, misted-over glass panel, the two lines flailing around inside the air-lock, curling around each other, separating, the shorn-off ends shining brightly… Thondup blinked, and was back with Gema.

He turned away from her, and stared at the figure lying in the recovery pod. "At a first glance, he looks intact." Thondup relaxed a little in his seat. "Perhaps the situation isn't that serious then..." He heard Gema's voice in the distance:

"I can't understand it... How could it have happened?"

"Palas must have become aware of the meteorite at the very last moment. It started the engines to change course..."

Gema interrupted him:

"That wouldn't have been enough to snap the lines, Thondup. Otherwise the acceleration would have been so great it would have killed us all."

Thondup turned to look again at Gema's face, scrutinizing it. "Could she have switched? That's bad. Hypersensitivity isn't want we need right now..." He started talking again, his voice expressionless:

"I haven't finished, Gema. Palas also activated the magnetic field at its maximum. That would provide sufficient thrust to snap ten lines, don't you think?"

Gema did not answer.

"How to tell her all the rest?" Thondup pulled at the suit material, trying to stretch it over his injured knee. "No use... I think I'll have to... No, not yet. That's the last resort." He looked again at Gema; she was crying silently. "Better for her to unburden herself."

Suddenly, she asked, "Is there no way we can rescue them? They couldn't have drifted too far yet... Is Alix still in contact with them?"

Thondup's hand came to a halt on his knee.

"I haven't been able to make contact with them. The transmitter is damaged too..." He took a deep breath, before going on. "Listen to me, Gema. The situation is far worse than you think: Alix is dead."

For two, three seconds Gema's look showed only astonishment. Then pain, comprehension, and more pain flashed across her face.

Thondup continued, his voice a whisper:

"Yes, it was difficult for me… But you needn't worry. I gathered up what was left of her, and put her in the refuse chute… That at least isn't damaged; it worked fine."

Gema had leapt forward in her seat, her eyes popping:

"You… *you did that?* Before even…?"

Her throat could not sustain so much tension, and her voice trailed off. She swallowed desperately, and went on hoarsely:

"Thondup, you could not have known whether she was really dead. Perhaps I could have…"

Something in Thondup's eyes silenced her. She understood: "*I gathered up what was left of her…* The meteorite must have smashed into the bridge…" She managed to erase the fleeting vision that had flashed through her mind, but her stomach was already heaving. She had to call on all her reserves of self-control to keep back the wave of nausea rising in her throat: slowly, slowly, it subsided…

"I understand. Thank you for your thoughtfulness, dear Thondup, but I don't know what is worse, seeing it… or imagining it."

Thondup was still observing her.

"She has recovered… but not completely. Enough though, I hope."

He said out loud, "There's more, Gema. Another fragment of the meteorite hit Palas' logic circuits. The bio-computer was on the point of completely disintegrating, but I was in time to readjust its homeostatic system and isolate the damaged area. We can still count on the auxiliary memories and the ultra-rapid calculation units, but we've lost the autopilot…"

As he spoke, Thondup did not take his eyes off Gema's changing expression. "No, I can't tell her yet. She needs more time to recover. Better for her to talk, that should calm her down."

"There is other news I have to give you... It's not good either, but first I'd like to know how he is." He pointed his chin towards Isanusi.

Before replying, Gema drew a hand across her face.

"Well... I'm not sure yet. I found him in the hypnotron, apparently still asleep. But I couldn't wake him; the apparatus did not respond. I lifted him out and brought him here, still unconscious. I put him in the diagnostic machine, but that wasn't working either. So I left him in the recovery pod, and waited. He woke up a short while ago. He couldn't see, move, or feel anything, although he could talk, and hear... I put him back to sleep. I can't determine what's wrong or how to cure him without more information. It's absolutely necessary for you to repair the diagnostic machine and find out what happened to the hypnotron, what it did to Isanusi, to know if it's possible..."

The end of her sentence was choked by a sob. Gema dried her eyes clumsily, then tried to continue:

"Although... if we are objective... we would... not count on..."

Her voice failed her completely. Her chin dropped to her chest. Her long hair veiled her face, which shook spasmodically. Thondup's lips stretched in a taut line: "Now what? There was obviously no way to avoid it... What can I do? I can't leave her like this, she's slipping towards hysteria... Disinhibit her?" Uncertain, he chewed his bottom lip. "There are three of us left. I can't count on Isanusi or on her. I have to make decisions on my own, and rapidly... There's no other way, so prepare yourself, Thondup." He concentrated for a full minute. "Now."

He projected his voice toward the figure slumped in her seat:

"*Gema!*"

It was little more than a whisper, but Thondup smiled with satisfaction. "The exact frequency." Next to him, the mass of black hair had stopped shaking. Gema was straightening up, pushing the hair back from her eyes, attempting a damp smile:

"I'm sorry I lost control, Thon—"

She did not finish. Her eyebrows shot up in surprise: "What's happened to me?" She perceived the new, strange fluidity of her thoughts. "Abnormally quick recuperation. Even before the crisis point was reached... How do you know this, Gema?" She peered inside herself. "I simply *know* it. I also know it will not happen again... Are you sure?" She deliberately demolished her internal psychoprotective barriers...

Pavel and Kay, floating in nothingness, with the spacecraft further and further away... The two of them floating apart as well. Their voices, calling to each other, to us... Enough air for three hours. Three hours...

She shook her head in disbelief. "Let's see." Another barrier was smashed to smithereens...

The bridge? Alix. What was left of her..."

She saw the horror, the terror, flooding past the previous limits of her resistance. "Strange the muffled way they reach me... No, in fact they aren't reaching me." Her forehead furrowed. "That's enough," she commanded; the phantoms and dim fears vanished. "What has happened to me?" Some incomprehensible words came floating into her mind:

"Conditioning for unexpected situations... What does that mean?" No answer. "Alright..." Gema felt no unpleasantness or fear, nothing but curiosity. "First of all, how did it happen? What caused it?" The answer came even before she had properly formulated the question: "It was Thondup. His voice, not what he said. The way he pronounced the syllables in my name... But why did he think he needed to activate the conditioning? We're in a difficult situation, but it's not desperate..." Then she remembered: *"more news, not good either...*" She nodded to herself. "Obviously, it's this other news that makes the situation desperate... Why didn't he tell me it before now?" She scrutinized the face of the man beside her. "He proceeded correctly. In my previous state, to tell me would have been... dangerous. But now he can tell me the news without any risk, so why doesn't he...? I understand; he's waiting for me to adapt." Against her will, the question returned: "What can this other news be?" Fragmentary images drifted into her mind: "Thirst. Blacking out. Nausea; the densiplasma ejector..." At a loss, she scanned her memory of the layout of *Sviatagor*. "Could this have something to do with it?" Yielding to the imperious necessity-order rising from the depths of her awareness, she studied the mental diagram. "The bridge. Alix was there... Then the laboratory. I was unconscious in there, until Thondup... and then, the nuclear reactor." The fragments coalesced, forming a unified whole. Gema breathed out, relieved she had found the answer.

"So that was it... Yes, Thondup was right. We have to..." Her mind went on steadily drawing conclusions. Gema leapt up, instinctively moving away from the recovery pod. Something akin to emotion made her voice tremble as she said to Thondup:

"Come on, let's get to the bridge at once..."

23:51 hours

The door opened noiselessly. Gema glanced rapidly around the bridge deck, taking in where the tangled cables were sticking out of smashed wall panels, the irregular patches of densiplasma covering the holes caused by the meteorite fragments... "It obviously exploded when it pierced the inner hull; Alix had no chance." She crossed the room, passing behind the captain's toppled chair. She noted the brown patches on the backrest and realized where they had come from. "We'll have to change the cover."

She halted in front of the main control panel, staring for a moment at the figures registered on the dials, and committed them to memory. She nodded absently. "Thondup was right. Palas had time to start the engines and change direction. He was successful, and we're moving out of the planetary plane and its elevated density... but also away from Earth. We need to set a fresh course." She was about to lose herself in the calculations, but remembered why she was there: "The new course can wait; there's still time." She put her hand into an opening in the main control panel. She had to lean over to reach the bottom. In this new position she could see on the floor a blob of white, sticky substance... She froze. "Is that from Alix? Probably." She bent down to examine this fresh challenge to her curiosity. "There's no doubt about it, it's brain matter... but it's not human; it must have belonged to Palas." Straightening up, she felt inside the control panel, and finally took out an icosahedron. She lifted it to her mouth:

"Gema reporting; today, at..."

The icosahedron began to vibrate in her hand. Her eyebrows shot up: "Why...?" It must have been set for Isanusi.

She added rapidly, "Emergency situation: Isanusi is physically incapacitated and cannot report." Instead of ceasing, the vibration spread uncomfortably through her whole body. "What am I not doing?" Something stirred deep in her consciousness, and the adequate response presented itself:

"His substitute Alix is dead."

"Is there anyone else? No; I'm number three in rank. I should have realized sooner..." Satisfied, the icosahedron gave off a faint glow.

"Continuing my report. At 18:03 hours, solar time, we collided with a meteorite. Reason: fault in the forward magnetic field inductor. Consequences: Palas' central logic circuits were destroyed. Pavel, Alix and Kay are dead. Isanusi is…"

"He's waking up, Gema."

She recognized the voice at once: Thondup. She looked over her shoulder to see where he was; there was no one else on the bridge.

The lab was visible through the open door. Nobody there either.

"Where is he?"

"The audio channel on the intercom is fixed. It will take me longer to restore the visual system…"

Force of habit led Gema to turn towards the empty screen and ask, "What about the diagnostic machine?"

She heard Thondup clear his throat.

"Impossible, Gema… Its integrator ran off Palas. But I discovered what happened to the hypnotron: an uncontrolled energy surge, which blew all the controls. The same happened to the transmitters and the receiver…"

Gema interrupted him:

"Thondup, our greatest concern now is the hypnotron. What happened to that excess energy?"

"It was diverted straight to Isanusi's nervous system … Fortunately, it must have been almost instantaneous; the conductors could not withstand it. We need to check what is left of them. Luckily, they did not resist for long; if they had, Isanusi would not be alive now. Hurry up: the pod is indicating a rapid rise in his conscious brain activity. I think he will be fully awake in less than two minutes."

"Fine. I'm coming."

She raised the throbbing icosahedron to her lips once more:

"For work reasons I am interrupting this report…"

She glanced quickly at the glowing dials, and concluded: "Until tomorrow."

One last pulse of light, and the icosahedron was extinguished.

Thursday December 30, 2038
00:06 hours

The material of his suit was rubbing painfully against his knee. Shifting in his seat, Thondup tried to find a more comfortable position. He ought to cut off the trouser leg... but the swelling should soon be going down; better to put up with it for now. "At least it's helping me stay awake..." He yawned. "But I still need to rest. Gema can give the report on her own, she's much better at it than me." He closed the lids over his red-rimmed eyes. He could hear Gema's voice clearly, but at first hardly bothered to listen. "She's not saying anything I don't already know... Although..." Suddenly he was all ears. "What's wrong? That isn't her normal voice, or the one corresponding to her new conditioning." He opened his eyes again. "She still hasn't got used to him not seeing her; she is controlling her facial expressions... Why? Is she trying to hide something from me? What could that be?"

By now he was wide-awake. He closely followed the inflections in Gema's voice. "No doubt about it, she's trying to keep something back. Not from me; it's obvious she's focused on Isanusi. What can she want to hide from him? His real state? Why? That's absurd. It makes no sense." Forgetting his knee, he straightened up in his seat to listen more intently:

"...all of that excess energy passed through your nerve receptors. I still need to do a biopsy to test the exact state of your neurons, but there's no doubt the peripheral system has been seriously affected, possibly for good..."

"No, it's not his state she's trying to hide from him... What then?"

"If you could remember something important, what you were dreaming when the crash happened, for example, if you can do that, I'm sure you'll be able to recall the exact moment it took place..."

Without realizing it, Thondup's hand fell onto his injured knee. He ignored the rush of pain, biting his lips, annoyed with himself. "Why didn't I think of that before? That must be the reason for the uneven effect on the sensory channels..."

His voice so hoarse it was almost unrecognizable, Isanusi began:

"I dreamt I was back on Earth."

An unintentional smile formed on Thondup's lips. "There was no need for him to say that. When don't we dream of Earth?" An absent look replaced his smile. "Yet when we have it beneath our feet again, if that were possible..." He frowned. "Attention, don't let your mind wander." He listened again.

"...instead of trying to skirt the ravine, I decided to jump across it. When I was in mid-air and had almost reached the far side, I felt... It 's hard to explain, Gema, but I'm sure that was the precise moment of the accident. It felt like my eyes, my whole body, were on fire."

Gema's head moved slowly up and down. She asked him again:

"Try to remember, Isanusi; the moment that happened, were you talking or listening to something?"

"That's obvious, but there's no harm verifying it. Naturally, the hypnotron only affected the nerves it was directly connected to."

Thondup interrupted his thoughts to hear Isanusi's reply:

"That's right, I wasn't talking or listening to anything. My body was tense, ready for hitting the ground... I also remember the sensation of a warm breeze on my skin... I was staring at a bush on the bank where I was going to land. I think I could still count every one of its leaves..."

Gema commented, betraying no emotion:

"Yes, it's all clear now."

There was a prolonged silence in the sick bay. Isanusi broke it by asking Gema:

"Have you concluded your report?"

"Yes."

Thondup glanced reprovingly towards Gema. She stared back at him... "So that was what she wanted to hide from him... But why? She told him straight out about his physical state... I don't understand." He lowered his eyes to the floor. "What shall I do now? If I intervene, I could disturb the balance of the group... What group?" He sighed. "Anyway, she has to be the one who corrects it..."

He suddenly realized Isanusi had been talking to him for some time, and blinked:

"I'm sorry, I wasn't listening. What were you saying?"

Her face expressionless, Gema interrupted him:

"Isanusi was saying that if that was all, why did you decide to activate my conditioning?"

She turned towards the pod before replying.

"He doesn't have to explain, Isanusi, I can." She took a deep breath. "As I told you, the meteorite disintegrated when it penetrated the flight deck. What I didn't tell you was that the largest piece pierced the partition between there and the laboratory. It crossed the entire room, and ended up embedded in the far wall, where the nuclear reactor is located. It didn't manage to get any farther, or we wouldn't be talking like this now, but it did make a deep gash in the protective shield. At that moment I was unconscious in the lab. I calculate that I was exposed to the radiation for about three minutes before Thondup arrived. Then we must have been in there for another four or five minutes... Then, while he was repairing the panels, Thondup discovered the hole. It's possible he wasn't exposed as long as I was, but when he was trying to repair it he had to get close, whereas I was on the far side of the lab the whole time... In any case, I don't possess the necessary elements to be able to assess the level of radiation we received. However, a rough estimate based on the symptoms and the residual radiation on our clothing suggests that it is quite likely it was a mortal dose."

For a few moments, Isanusi's lips moved without making a sound... Eventually he asked:

"Gema, is it possible to make any assessment of the injuries you suffered?"

"Not right now. We need to study how Thondup and I evolve over the coming days... If we could adapt the microanalyzer to study our blood composition, we could reach a trustworthy prognosis in say, five or six days... Not before then."

Another pause, then the leader of the Titan group spoke once more:

"There's no doubt the situation is dangerous, and will only get more so... But we mustn't lose sight of the essential: *Sviatagor* has to return to Earth, whatever the losses we have suffered or are likely to face. Let's examine our possibilities: Palas has been destroyed, Alix is dead, and I am physically out of action. But thanks to her conditioning, Gema can take our place satisfactorily... Of course, we can't forget the problem of radioactive contamination you two have, which means we can't make any definitive plans until we know what the real chances are of you surviving. We will have to wait until we know that... but in the meantime, there's work to be done, a lot of work. First of all, we have to rebuild the ship's protective system. It's true we've moved out of the plane of greatest material density around the sun, but that doesn't mean the space we are travelling through has no density. Even though it's not so likely, there still exists the possibility of another collision with a meteorite. Thondup, you need to connect the radiodetection system to one of Palas' surviving memory systems and program it so that *Sviatagor* alters course as soon as it detects any object in our path... Gema, you work out a new trajectory for approaching the Earth. Not directly though. Try to make sure we travel parallel to the planetary plane; otherwise, you'll have to continually correct the direction. Don't forget we are drawing close to the asteroid belt..."

"I can't forget that, Isanusi."

Isanusi's eyebrows seemed to indicate assent.

"I'm the one who forgets sometimes... Let's continue. Now that we no longer have Palas, you'll have your work cut out with me, studying Thondup and yourself, maintaining the nutrient crops and living conditions on board... But you need to reserve some time to think as well..." Isanusi had a coughing fit. It took him some time to get his breath back and go on:

"To think what we could do in the worst possible scenario in order to guarantee that *Sviatagor* gets back... Thondup, you will have to sort out the anti-meteorite protective shield, adapt the microanalyzer, and repair everything it is humanly possible to repair. We have no idea what we might need to accomplish our mission. In addition, you'll have to periodically check all the installations. There is no Palas to advise us when anything fails... You have a possibility that any psychosociologist would envy: to study Gema in her new state and observe how well it works. Don't let it go to waste. We'll see which of you was right... And you also need to think. The present situation is throwing up sociological factors that are bound to affect us…" He paused for a longer time to draw breath. Then he went on: "Which are already affecting us." He attempted a smile, and managed a reasonable approximation. He asked, "What time is it, Gema?"

She had no need to look up at the clock in the wall:

"It's 00:23 hours."

"So late? You need to rest… But first you have to repair the protective shield, Thondup. Without it, we might never wake up again."

Thondup smiled mechanically.

Isanusi concluded:

"You can leave."

Thondup and Gema stood up together.

"Not you, Gema." The young woman came to a halt halfway between the pod and the door. "I still need to talk to you…"

00:25 hours

Thondup leaned cautiously against the corridor wall, waiting for the mist to disperse. "Don't give in to temptation; don't have another blackout, or you won't last three days… Stay calm." He let his back slide down the wall until he was seated on the floor. "Take this opportunity to think, Thondup. Several things happened in the meeting with Isanusi that you weren't able to foresee… and that you still don't understand, admit it. Why didn't Gema want to mention the radiation we received to Isanusi? That doesn't make sense. Theoretically, her conditioning should prevent her actions from being affected by emotion, or any kind of subjective factor… Even accepting the improbable hypothesis that she preserved emotional factors in her mental structures, what she tried to keep from Isanusi was the seriousness of her own physical state... No, I can't make out the answer. Better try to see whether I can carry on." He struggled to his feet. "I can't work like this... I'll have to talk to Gema and suggest she reduces the gravity to 0.8G. That would make it easier to move around..." He stood away from the wall, testing the strength of his legs: "Yes, I can do it." He suddenly straightened up. A face he knew only too well was floating in front of him, smiling... "Go away!" Alix's features dissolved back into the air they had emerged from, leaving only the green walls of the corridor. "Get to work, don't waste any more time." He limped as quickly as he could towards the bridge... "It shouldn't take long, an hour at most, and then I can sleep... I really need it." He stopped, short of breath. He leaned with all his weight against the closest wall, waiting for the trembling in his legs to cease. "There's no need to go so quickly... I'm almost at the lab. How did Isanusi realize that Gema had been disinhibited? She was speaking normally, perhaps more dryly than usual, but that could have been taken as a natural reaction... Is Isanusi able to interpret voices? I've never seen him do that before... But there's never been such a crisis before either. Yes, he must have used the vocal timbres to find out. And he took it as something normal; I would never have been able to... But he has his own view of the effects of conditioning; I hope I'm the one who's mistaken... Anyway, he still has Gema alive, whereas I..." A pair of infinitely precious lips appeared in the air on front of him, quivering as if about to speak. "Be careful, Thondup!" Alix's mouth vanished. Thondup ran his tongue over his dry lips. "I don't like what I'm seeing... I'll have to redouble my self-control. It's important to save energy, but my mental health is even more crucial." He concentrated on a vague point somewhere beyond the far wall of the corridor. His breathing slowed and became weaker, while in his mind he brought up the key images in rapid succession. The exterior world ceased to exist; Thondup plunged dizzily into his vast interior universe... He filled his thought processes with his willpower and projected them to unknown depths. "NO MORE VISIONS." As quickly as he could, before it was too late, he shot back up to reality, to the dimly-lit corridor of the spacecraft... He waited a few minutes, his mind empty of all thoughts, until his strength returned. Then he hobbled resolutely towards the bridge of the stricken vessel.

01:39 hours

He stretched the thin cable all along the wall, gently pressing it in. When he let go, the static charge kept it tightly in place. He adjusted the terminals at the entrance to the engine controls. "Ready." He went slowly over to the memory unit, juggling thoughtfully with the tiny cube containing the program. "Will one degree of deviation be enough? Or would two be better? Gema must be asleep by now, I can't consult her..." He halted next to the memory store, thinking it over. "One will do. If a meteorite is still headed towards us, the system will be activated again, and change course another degree... Yes, that's best... It reduces energy use to the minimum, both to avoid the collision and for any future adjustments to our trajectory." He slipped the cube into the memory store. "And now, to get some rest. As Audo used to say: 'To sleep, perchance to dream...' No, I'd better avoid dreams." He crossed the deck walking almost normally. "The knee is getting better... My thirst, though, is getting worse. He was already in the lab. He went over to the dining table. When he touched one edge, the long cylindrical hydrophore emerged. He put it to his lips and sucked greedily. The cool water eased his burning mouth a little. Letting the hydrophore slide back down into its cavity, he half-heartedly read the card that had appeared in the center of the table. He shook his head: "No, I'm not hungry." He moved out into the corridor, on the way to his cabin. "Tomorrow my first task is to adjust the microanalyzer... then I'll see what can be done with the transmitter." His footsteps resounded in the empty corridor. "How lonely the spaceship is now..." He became aware of the sound of familiar footsteps mixed with his own. He halted. He turned to look over his shoulder: the corridor was empty.

"Gema?"

Silence. He smiled: "Of course, there's no one there... Who were you expecting to see, you idiot?" He renewed his walk and once again heard the whisper of someone else's steps. This time he did not come to a stop but listened more closely, carefully analyzing the quiet sounds... He let out his breath. "What else could it be but the echo of my own footsteps?" He pinched his lips together. "You really have to be careful with your imagination, Thondup." He opened the door and entered his cabin. The light had come on automatically. He looked at his bed—his and Alix's—too wide now. He sighed and started to undress. "I wonder what tomorrow has in store for us?" He carefully felt his injured knee, noting the visible reduction in the swelling: "It's much better... It's probable the group will suffer fresh losses... It's almost certain, whatever may happen; and the awareness of earlier losses will become all the sharper, as time goes by... Alix, Alix." He struggled to repress the sob rising in his throat. "As someone... who...? I don't remember: But it was, and is very true: a group is superbly effective, as long as it doesn't suffer any mutilations..." He went into the bathroom: the door closed automatically behind him.

"Yes, the losses have been really severe… And what's left? Isanusi out of action, close to death, and Gema has been turned into a human computer… That was absolutely necessary; even Isanusi had agreed. But that was because he couldn't see her face, and her… heuristic expression… Yes, we've lost Gema too: so what's left?" He dried his face and left the bathroom. "What's happening to me? These aren't the kind of thoughts I should be having… I see, it's a reaction. Self-control has its limits." There was a knocking at the door. A shiver ran down Thondup's spine. "Who…? It can only be Gema. Unless it's another auditory delusion…" He waited, his eyes fixed on the door. The knocking started again. "What are you waiting for? Open it. If it's a delusion, it doesn't matter; there simply won't be anyone on the other side of the door…" and yet he stood there, trembling. The handle creaked. "I didn't lock it." He was about to leap towards it, but the door was already opening… Gema was staring at him from the threshold. She asked, in her expressionless voice:

"Can I come in?"

Thondup nodded; he was unable to speak. Gema entered the room. Without looking at him, she began to get undressed. Taken aback, Thondup sat on the edge of the bed. He said faintly:

"What are you doing?"

One of the magnetic fasteners at the side of her suit was proving hard to undo. Peering down at it, Gema replied:

"You wouldn't want me to sleep in my clothes, would you? It's not hygienic."

Thondup's eyes opened wider.

"You're intending to sleep here? It's not right, Gema."

The fastener finally gave way. Raising her cold, curious eyes to him, Gema said, as if to herself:

"It seems Isanusi was right…"

"You mean he knew you were coming here?"

Gema had disappeared into the bathroom. She replied from there:

"He was the one who wanted me to sleep here... I'd better play you his message."

Gema's voice became an almost exact replica of Isanusi's hoarse whisper:

"Thondup, you've shown how well your self-control works. But there are limits to everything... You need to avoid loneliness and its phantoms for your own good. Let Gema keep you company. If I'm wrong and have underestimated your resistance, you can send her to her own cabin. Get some rest."

Gema's normal voice returned, and she concluded. "Apparently he wasn't wrong."

She came out of the bathroom, smoothing down her hair. Her face showed something close to concern. "Two liquid stools in a little more than six hours... It could be worse. How many have you had?"

"Three," replied Thondup mechanically. Gema sat down on the bed beside him.

"You need to take in more liquids. The danger of dehydration..."

Thondup did not let her finish:

"Gema, when Isanusi sent you here to sleep with me, did he also program you to have relations with me?"

Gema looked surprised.

"He didn't say anything about that. I suppose he left it up to me."

She judged the state Thondup was in.

"Taking into account how you look now, I don't think you're capable of doing anything today. Tomorrow perhaps, should you consider it nec—"

—Thondup's right arm traced a wide arc towards Gema's face.

She raised her forearm quickly and blocked the blow. They sat for a long while in silence, staring at each other, until at last Gema said:

"I don't understand you, Thondup."

The man nodded reluctantly.

"I'm beginning to think I don't understand you either, Gema."

Getting up from the bed, she asked:

"So do I have to leave?"

Thondup shuddered.

"No, stay." He gave a forced smile. "I suspect I'm not thinking or acting normally... Yes, Isanusi was right."

"Good... Let's go to bed. Which side did Alix sleep on?"

"On the inside; get in." Thondup moved, and Gema crawled across the bed to her side. She settled down, and said:

"You can switch the light off, if you like."

Thondup looked at her warily. Gema was lying flat on her back, her body stiff and her eyes open, unblinking. He asked her:

"Doesn't the light bother you if you want to sleep?"

"I don't need to sleep now."

"So when will you?"

"I don't know."

Lying on his side facing Gema, he propped himself up on his elbow and asked:

"So what are you doing?"

"Thinking."

"About what?"

"About what we could do, in the worst of cases, to make sure that *Sviatagor* returns to earth."

Thondup frowned.

"Please, when you're quoting Isanusi, do it in your own voice."

"If that's what you want..."

Thondup could feel the arm he was leaning on going to sleep. He turned until he was lying on his back, still looking at Gema. She didn't move.

"Have you reached any conclusion?" Thondup let out a sigh. "It's like talking to Palas." He thought: "Now I can clear up my doubt."

"Gema..."

"What is it?"

"Can you tell me why you tried to keep our radioactive contamination from Isanusi?"

The young woman took some time to reply.

"I don't know."

"Think harder; there must have been a reason. According to your conditioning... You do know you've been conditioned, don't you?"

"Yes."

"According to that, as I said, there is no reason to hide information of any kind when any of us asks you a question. So how is it possible that you tried to do so?"

"I don't know."

Thondup's patience was at an end.

"But how...?" He controlled himself, and lowered his voice to almost a whisper. "Try to remember, Gema. You were with me and Isanusi. You were informing him about the state he was in, in which the Titan group is. Didn't you feel the need to tell him absolutely everything?"

"Yes."

Thondup sat up eagerly in the bed.

"You also felt the need to tell him that, didn't you?"

"Yes, I did."

"So what happened? And please, not another 'I don't know.'"

Gema hesitated. She glanced at Thondup, and said:

"I understand what you want, Thondup... But all I can tell you is that there was something inside me that prevented me from communicating that to Isanusi."

"Only that? Why didn't it stop you telling him other things, his real physical state for example?"

"I don't... I don't know the reason."

With a groan, Thondup collapsed onto his back. Gema reached out and laid her hand on his arm.

"Thondup, please... Don't go on asking me about that. Each time you insist and I realize I can't give you a satisfactory answer, I feel bad."

Eyes closed, Thondup waved his agreement. "Right, obviously. The basic principle of dealing with computers: If you don't know something, don't insist, because it could seriously damage their circuits. This isn't Gema beside me, it's Palas." He turned his back on her, roughly pushing off her hand. "That's enough questions; I'm wasting my time. Alix, Alix, I need you so much... but it's a thousand times better knowing you're dead rather than converted into something like this."

A timid but urgent hand was touching his back. He asked gruffly:

"What do you want now?"

Gema's voice trembled as she asked:

"Thondup, I still feel bad. I can't concentrate and continue thinking, as I ought to be doing... Couldn't you ask me another question I was able to answer?"

Thondup did not move or reply. "If I had imagined this before... Not even if it had been our only hope would I have started her conditioning." He could hear her anxious breathing at his back. "I don't care; I'm not lifting a finger to help her."

"Please…"

Turning towards her, Thondup looked at her angrily. Silent tears were welling in Gema's eyes.

"Alright; tell me, who was the first man who slept with you?"

Gema smiled.

"Audo. Thank you, Thondup."

Her face and body visibly relaxed. Thondup lay openmouthed, unable to take his eyes off her… He recovered, and asked:

"Does Isanusi know?"

"Of course…" Half sitting up in the bed, Gema was watching him curiously. "In the end, Alix was right. You still retain the prejudices of the land you were born in. That's surprising…" She caught her breath. "Now I understand the real meaning behind your question: you were trying to hurt me, not help me. Why?"

Thondup seized her by the shoulders.

"Tell me, who was the first for Alix?"

"I don't… She never told me."

Thondup's hands pressed into her shoulder blades.

"Look, I can analyze tones of voice. I can tell when people are lying and when they are telling the truth… and you weren't. Was it Audo?"

"No, not him."

"Who then…?"

"Thondup, you're harming yourself."

"I *want* to harm myself. What did she tell you?"

The expression on Gema's face slowly transformed. Thondup's hands slipped from her shoulders. "That way she has of twisting her lip… No!"

He heard Alix's voice, whispering to Gema:

"Gema, I'd like to talk to you…"

"That's enough!"

Burying his face in the bed, Thondup started crying. Gema's hand moved gently up and down his back. Without raising his head, Thondup murmured:

"Forgive me, Gema."

"What for? You didn't do anything to me... But if that's what you want, I forgive you. Calm down though..."

"I feel so ashamed, Gema: all of my worst side came spilling out."

"If it came out, so much the better; don't let it find its way back inside. And now, sleep... rest... it's very late..."

Gema kept repeating soothing words like a lullaby, her warm hand stroking the man's back long after Thondup had fallen asleep.

09:20 hours

"And that was all?"

"Yes."

"And when he woke up?"

"First of all he looked at me in surprise. Then he said good morning, in a perfectly normal manner. He was smiling, but I'm not sure that reflected his true state of mind. He went into the bathroom, spent about five minutes in there, and came out fully dressed. He told me he was going to adjust the microanalyzer, and went out."

Isanusi's lips plumped up. "The crisis was worse than I thought... But what else was going to happen? He had controlled himself too much; he was the one affected the most. At least I have Gema, and Gema..."

He asked: "How do you feel?"

She blinked.

"Well... Insecure."

"Why? Explain yourself. I don't know what you mean."

With an old, almost forgotten gesture, Gema pulled at her lower lip before replying:

"Isanusi, when I have to deal with figures or any kind of problem, I can easily find a solution. It's as if it comes to me naturally... But when I'm dealing with Thondup, and sometimes even with you, I find I don't understand. I cannot detect the logic system behind what is being said or what is being done, and yet I know it must exist..."

"I understand... You have to be patient, Gema. You're still adapting to your new... to your new characteristics. Until you can control them properly, you're going to find it difficult."

"But that's not all, Isanusi. I've come to the conclusion that Thondup doesn't think I'm human."

"He's mistaken, Gema. He's been badly hit by the loss of Alix, and that has affected his powers of judgment."

"There's another example of what I mean... If she's dead, what can he do about it? Why does he torture himself so? It's not logical."

Isanusi sighed.

"The time will come when you understand..." A sudden stab of pain took his breath away. "What if I were the one mistaken? No, no, that can't be... I simply have to help her." He went on: "You still have stored all the memories from before your new state; there's enough material there for you to comprehend our way of behaving. Study them, and you'll see..."

Gema nodded, unconvinced.

"Yes, I do remember, and far more clearly now, but I still don't understand... As I was being conditioned, I could still understand, but that has become hazier and hazier, until it has disappeared... Perhaps I didn't pay enough attention, Isanusi."

"That's probable... After all, you've been too busy adapting to your new capabilities to be able to pay enough attention to your old ones. But you shouldn't just jettison them, Gema. Try to develop them in parallel, to make a new whole out of them..." By now Isanusi was exhausted and fell silent. "I have to save energy; I still need to tell her... Thondup should help her; he can." He heard Gema's expressionless voice.

"What you just told me... is that a task?"

"Yes."

"I'm not sure I have sufficient elements to be able to perform it."

"Talk to Thondup... He can explain to you what your conditioning means, and that will help you."

"Alright. Anything else?"

"No."

"May I withdraw then? Thondup must have fixed the microanalyzer by now. I have to analyze the samples from your nervous system and from our blood, then rectify *Sviatagor*'s course..."

"Yes, you may go."

11:45 hours

Thondup strode into the sick bay and asked:

"Are you awake, Isanusi?"

"Yes, what's happened?"

"I have to warn you: in a few minutes Gema will start the engines. She doesn't think it will affect you, but as a precaution..."

"I understand."

Thondup swiveled the pod and secured it to the nearest wall. He surveyed its new position and said, "Good... The acceleration will affect you from your head down, Isanusi. It won't be too severe, less than one G. That won't disturb you, will it?"

"I don't think so."

Thondup swiftly moved a chair to the side of the pod. Sitting down, he said, "I'll be at your side until Gema has finished. If there's anything you need, just tell me."

"That's fine. Thank you, Thondup."

"We can talk while we're waiting, if you like…"

"Talking tires me… Tell me about what you've done this morning."

Thondup leaned against the headrest, and began his report:

"First, I adjusted the microanalyzer. It wasn't difficult, but it took some time… Then I inspected the atmosphere control; it's working fine. I went on to check the damaged pieces of equipment, to see if any of them could be repaired… The transmitter can, but only for short distances. The directional antenna is useless; they will have to get used to having no news from us back on Earth."

Isanusi's brows furrowed.

"That's bad news, Thondup; I was counting on the transmitter."

"Me too… After that, I checked the receiver. I think something can be done with it. I had started dismantling it when Gema called me to say she was going to correct *Sviatagor*'s trajectory and needed me to test the controls. I looked at the engine connections, the inductor for the magnetic panels and the ejector, then I came here."

"You didn't get much done, did you, Thondup?"

"No, that's true. Under normal circumstances I could have managed twice as much… But if I have to pause every five minutes because I can't see and my head isn't clear, I suppose it's enough.

Not to mention the number of times I've had to go to the bathroom… It's impossible to work like this, Isanusi. I only hope that tomorrow we'll feel better; that's what Gema told me."

"Didn't she say anything more?"

Thondup hesitated for a moment.

"Yes, she did... She asked me to explain how she had been conditioned. Do you think that's a good idea?"

"Yes."

"But... Isanusi, I can't explain to her that we've changed her into a thinking machine; I'm not so insensitive."

"Do you still think that... I thought that what had happened in your meeting would have convinced you to the contrary."

Thondup peered warily at the figure inside the pod.

"Are you referring to...?"

A slight pressure pushed him back against the headrest. He fell silent, waiting for the engines to finish their silent thrust...

He turned abruptly towards Isanusi:

"Come on, explain..." He remembered why he was there: "Are you feeling alright?"

"Yes, but have you still not understood why she didn't want to mention your radiation problem to me?"

"No, and I've racked my brains trying to, believe me."

"She was trying to protect me."

Thondup shook his head.

"No. I admit I thought that for a moment, Isanusi, but it's not logical. If she had wanted to avoid upsetting you because of her feelings for you, she would have hidden how seriously ill you are."

Isanusi took a deep breath.

"Thondup, she could not stop me being aware of the state I am in, so from her current viewpoint, there was no reason to try to hide it."

Thondup thought for a moment... then concluded,

"That's too complicated."

"Do you have another explanation?"

"No… but that goes directly against the group protective principle inculcated into us through the conditioning. By giving you only partial information, you could have come up with a mistaken plan of action if you hadn't realized she had not told you everything… And that could have led to the failure of the entire expedition. There has to be another reason, Isanusi."

"Then find one." Isanusi thought: "They knew what they were doing when they didn't appoint you as an analyst, Thondup… Let's try again. "Thondup, the conditioning did not do away with all her previous modes of behavior. Of course, the ones that were directly against it had to be destroyed, but of any of them could be adapted to her new mental framework, then doubtless they were. So the old system and the new one merged, mutually reinforcing each other…"

Isanusi fell silent. He was panting. His lips moved, forming the same word over and over… Thondup translated:

"Water?"

Isanusi closed his eyes in assent. Thondup pressed the controls on the pod until the hydrophore emerged. He raised it to Isanusi's mouth, and kept it there until water began to seep from the corners of his mouth, then withdrew it. Thondup sat down again, deep in thought. Inside the pod, a lining rose along the path of the moist patch, and dried Isanusi's lips… After a few moments, the leader of the Titan group renewed his explanation:

"That's why I want her to know what happened in as much detail as possible… Knowing that, she will herself be able to help along the fusion between her old personality and her new one."

Thondup made up his mind to speak:

"Isanusi, last night I asked her about the reasons for her attitude when she was giving you her report… She had no idea. How does that fit in with your explanation?"

"All these processes take place at a level inside her that she is not aware of, because she doesn't know it exists... The conditioning has created immense possibilities for her, but if they are not trained, or directed..."

Thondup nodded.

"I understand. Or rather, I think I do... I will try to help her, Isanusi."

From inside the pod, he heard, faintly,

"Thank you, Thondup."

14:43 hours

There was a sound on the far side of the door. Rousing himself from his stupor, Isanusi listened hard: "It's being opened." Something whirred towards him and he heard light footsteps. "Gema ... and she's bringing something in a transporter."

"Welcome..." he murmured.

Gema came to a halt next to the pod.

She said, "I thought you were asleep... Well, it's better this way." She brought the floating transporter close to him and opened it, still speaking:

"The results of your neurological examination are complete. There is no great damage to the brain itself. The affected areas can be restored in a relatively short time... The peripheral system on the other hand is severely hit; the nerve endings will not recuperate, at least not under present conditions."

She paused to fill the transparent container. The yellowish liquid inside had been shaken up as it was transported to the pod, but now it was settling, as was Gema's breathing.

"Your nerve endings are dying… and this process isn't limited to the currently affected area: it could travel throughout the nervous system and reach the brain. I've brought…" She tapped the container with her fingernail. "…a solution I've prepared. Its main component should remain in the dead nervous tissue, isolating it from the sections that are still healthy. I calculate that this could be painful, and so I have added an anesthetic that will render you unconscious while the treatment is taking effect. I have to warn you that this first dose will last twenty-four hours…" She found a vein in his arm and picked up the needle. "If there's something you want to say before I begin, I'm listening." She waited a moment.

"Until tomorrow then."

The needle entered his vein at the first attempt.

18:16 hours

Thondup moved the spoon listlessly around his plate… then pushed it away from him.

"Don't you want any more? Didn't you like it?"

He pulled a face before replying:

"The taste isn't bad… but I can't force it down my throat."

Gema nodded, feeling guilty.

"I should have foreseen it." She pushed her own almost untouched plate of food away as well. "Anorexia is another typical symptoms… I'll make something more suitable tomorrow, Thondup."

Thondup took a long drink from the hydrophore and tried to stand up. He couldn't. He sighed:

"I'm exhausted, Gema. I doubt if I could walk five steps without falling. What shall I do?"

"Rest. For two or three hours... three, preferably."

"Impossible. You yourself asked me to verify the nutrient plant module, as well as the thermoregulator: I've noticed the temperature has been lower than normal for some time now. Besides, I'd like to start repairing the receiver... Couldn't you give me another dose, Gema?"

"It's not recommended. After resting for three hours, you'll be able to work for one; only at half-speed, of course. And then, a proper sleep. Don't worry about the thermoregulator; it's your fever that makes it seem cold."

"If you say so... Where can I rest? Not far from here, if you want me to get there."

"We could rest here; I need to as well."

"I can't stand the sight of food..."

Gema gathered up the plates and placed them in the center of the table. She pressed a button, and they slid slowly inside it.

Thondup shifted uncomfortably in his seat. "Three hours: what can I do for all that time?" He remembered his conversation with Isanusi:

"Gema, can we talk?"

"We can."

"Good. Didn't you want me to tell you about the conditioning?"

Color flowed to the young woman's face.

"I was afraid you had forgotten about that."

"As you see, I hadn't... Let's start at the very beginning: suggestocybernetics. It emerged in the last twenty-five years..."

Gema's mouth opened as if she was about to speak, but then closed again without a sound. "He could be offended if I told him I know all this already."

"...unjustified hopes that once everyone was trained, they could all learn everything... but with the spread of the method beyond laboratory conditions, its limitations became obvious. Yes, it was a way to teach everyone languages, geography... well, things that could be memorized. But in other areas that demanded conscious comprehension, suggestocybernetics achieved only limited results. Eventually they discovered the reason..."

"It must be the fever; I don't recall ever having seen him so talkative, so vague..."

"... the assimilation of complex topics depended on the complexity of cognitive patterns created by individuals prior to the application of the suggestocybernetic methods... To put it more clearly, yes, and more precisely, only concepts as complex or less complex than the thought process of the person being submitted to these methods could be assimilated..."

Digging deep in her memory, Gema wondered, "What would Audo do in my case...? Raising his arms to the skies, he would say: 'My goodness!...' Yes, the method Isanusi suggested seems effective."

"... solution; to utilize the methods of suggestocybernetics to implant not only knowledge, but also cognitive patterns not previously acquired..."

Gema automatically paid attention: "This was not in my memory."

"... first experiments carried out at the end of the last century were inevitably destined to fail..." Thondup paused to drink some water. He left the hydrophore on the table and apologized. "My throat was so dry... Where was I?"

Gema hastily replied,

"... inevitably destined to fail. That was where you had reached..."

"Thanks... Yes, they failed. That was because there was not yet sufficient knowledge of the physiochemical basis of thought, not to mention its intrinsic structure. So the classic tools of suggestocybernetics had about as much chance of implanting new cognitive patterns as an arrow of reaching the Moon..."

"Kay would have put her head down on the table and pretended she was snoring... Mmm, not so sure about that, I'd better try Alix ..."

"... and Vogel, the creators of the mental field theory, together with the neuroinductors developed by the collective headed by Stasenko, made possible the first experiments with human beings ..."

Gema straightened up, the leaned forward, all ears now.

"...using a gradual approach, that is, implanting one new basic thought pattern at a time, and then studying how it integrated with the cognitive system previously developed by the subject. The results were, frankly, discouraging; either the newly introduced pattern disintegrated and failed to function, cancelled out by the old way of thinking, or the existing pattern was displaced by the implanted one and ceased to operate. In the most extreme cases, typical schizophrenic symptoms appeared. This was only to be expected; the experiments had violated the principle that any individual's thought was not simply the arithmetical sum of the cognitive patterns acquired during their lifetime, but was the result of the interaction between all of them, developed over time, and unique to each case ..." He paused again for another drink. Afterwards, he remained silent, staring into the distance... Gema plucked up the courage to ask:

"And what happened after that, Thondup?"

"Eh? Oh... After what?"

"After the 'first experiments with human beings.'"

Thondup leaned back in his chair, lost in thought.

"Yes, now I remember... Naturally enough, in the Federation they immediately suspended all experiments of that nature. It was understood that to intervene in mankind's cognitive system meant to intervene, to affect his very personality, his individual consciousness ... But for the Empire, which had just been born, that was not fundamental. They were enthusiastic about the possibilities of neuroinductors: they might turn out to be the key to ensuring the stability of the system… Nothing easier than to implant new patterns of thought massively in those who refused to conform, in those who were too aware. The process left no traces…"

Gema was scrutinizing Thondup's reddened face. Without him noticing, she gently touched his hand. "His fever isn't that high, so what's going on?" The image of a densely packed tree diagram came to mind. "Yes, delirium is another symptom of radioactive poisoning."

"…from neuroinductors they produced multiple systems based on them: the psychosimulator you surely know of, the hypnotron, so useful on space voyages to guarantee the psychological stability of the travelers through the Cosmos… But as with any important discovery, this had two aspects, depending on who was applying it. That is where the permanent artificial paradises come in, those well-known 'Imperial Dream Palaces'…"

"Thondup, you were telling me about conditioning."

He looked at her. His eyes were slightly bloodshot.

"You're right… That was another application developed under the Empire. Thanks to trials carried out on prisoners, they understood that the implantation of mental patterns would only be successful—that is, produce individuals who could be integrated into society in the desired way—if complete systems of thought were introduced, not isolated patterns. In other words, it was necessary to completely annul the previous personality…"

"Should I give him a psychodepressor?… No, a psychostabilizer would be better. That way his reaction will put him to sleep… But first, I need to know."

"Thondup, I admit all this is very interesting. But what I want to know is why the conditioning was applied to me, not how it was developed under the Empire."

Thondup's troubled eyes slipped down her face and strayed around the walls of the relaxation-room.

"I was coming to that ..." He thumped the table. "In the Federation we did not carry out that kind of experiment on human beings. But the process had been studied a lot, and so we had more than enough material we could use. We had rescued several conditioned people from the Empire... We had to do all we could to turn them back into human beings. When we tried to erase the implanted thought processes, we ended up with vegetables in human form. Their previous personalities had not been overlaid by the conditioning; they had been completely wiped out. The only solution was to utilize the memories kept by those people who knew them before they had been conditioned to build approximate psychoprofiles, which were then implanted. In that way we achieved something closer to the men and women they had once been ..."

"Wouldn't it have been better to leave them as they were? I mean, in their conditioned state?"

Thondup's face darkened.

"Gema, you've never seen someone conditioned by the Empire ..." He fell silent, lost in his own thoughts. Gema insisted again:

"But why was I conditioned, Thondup?"

Startled, the man looked at her and blinked.

"You ...? Oh yes, I remember: because of the decadence of the human race. We are too sensitive, too impressionable ... In medieval times, women went to public executions, keen to see charred flesh, to hear the cries of those being tortured ... And afterwards they conversed animatedly, praising or criticizing the executioner's art, discussing subtle details of how to quarter, torture, kill people ... That's how our ancestors were, Gema, but we are nothing like them ... Studies were made of expeditions that never returned, and it was plain that a high percentage of the failures were due to our deep-seated inability to witness and assimilate with the proper indifference the agonizing deaths of our colleagues. Sometimes, as with the Ganymede expedition, the rest of the group rushed blindly to their own deaths, trying to save someone who could not be saved.

On other occasions, such as the Rustán expedition, the group controlled itself and allowed the inevitable to happen. But even though they knew it was impossible to do anything for the others—even understanding that—they were unable to retain their emotional stability. They felt remorse that they knew was absurd and illogical, but they felt it nevertheless. And sooner or later, a mistake was made that would have been unthinkable in their normal state: one of them switched off the surface insulation, or broke the thermoregulator, or something else, and the survivors all died during their return trip. Yes, the Cosmos demands a lot from those who seek to conquer it: a strong moral sense, deep feelings of comradeship, and generous, passionate instincts… and that's where it sets its ultimate trap. It demands that we are united as one, but that means it doesn't have to make any great effort to destroy us all at once. It's enough to snare two, or even just one; the rest will follow them to their deaths, faithful to the last…"

"Thondup, we were talking about my conditioning."

"Were we? Let's continue then… I'm sorry, I don't recall what I was saying…"

"You were just explaining the reasons why expeditions were lost."

"That's right. So how could this be counteracted? By weakening the bonds of friendship in the cosmogroups? Definitely not; we only had to look at what happened to the imperial expeditions when they faced a difficulty. No, that path led to even more rapid self-destruction … The psychosociologists racked their brains trying to discover how to increase the safety margin of expeditions. Trying to find a solution to that and also to the question of confronting unexpected challenges that seemed insurmountable. Not even Palas could resolve them... The only solution was to equip every ship with universal cyberbrains like Proteus. A Proteus is capable of analyzing every possible variable at the greatest possible speed, and choosing the best option... But because of its size and energy requirements, it cannot be installed in our spacecraft, and so for now we have to make do with the cyberpilots... It seemed impossible to eliminate the dangers, and inevitable that the loss of some members of the crew or the appearance of an unexpected problem would lead to an entire expedition being lost. That is until the Djelmar collective made its suggestion..."

Thondup felt on the table for the hydrophore. "Using the psychological profiles, in each group it is established which members are most likely to lose their emotional stability faced with the death of their companions. These crewmembers are conditioned in a latent way—in other words, the conditioning takes place at the level of the subconscious..."

He paused to drink. Then he went on: "...a new system of thought processes, which is inhibited as long as no conflictive situation arises ... If one does, they are disinhibited; their uncontrollable emotional reactions disappear, and there is no danger that a crisis will threaten the safety of the expedition. The other crewmembers will have universal bio-computers that allow them to find a solution, if there is one. That was how the problem was presented to us—to Isanusi, Kay, and myself. According to the authorities at the Academy, we were the most stable. They asked us if we agreed that the others—that is, you—were to be given the conditioning that they had created based on the logico-rational system found in the cyberbrain Proteus II. At first I was against it; I was horrified at the idea of Alix being converted into a computer…" He cast a sideways glance at Gema and muttered between clenched teeth: "Now more than ever." Then he said out loud: "In the end, they convinced me. The conditioning would be activated only in situations of extreme gravity, when the life of the whole crew was at risk. And if we managed to solve the problem and return to Earth, then they had the profiles of all of you. It would not take them long to re-implant them, give us our old companions back alive and sane. In short, it was all for your own good…"

"So why didn't they consult us as well? I don't think the idea would have upset me…"

Half-rising from his chair, Thondup pointed at her:

"Perhaps not you, but the others might have been. Knowing they had another personality inside their minds would have seriously affected them. At least that was what the modeling of their reactions in the psychosimulator indicated…" He dropped back into his seat, visibly exhausted. He went on talking, as if only to himself: "I regret it now. If Alix had survived, I would have found it unbearable to see her…"

He raised his eyes: "to see her like you."

"So how is it that Isanusi can bear me?"

A weary smile appeared on Thondup's lips.

"Isanusi, Isanusi… However good an analyst he may be, and even though he thinks he can see much further, he's no psychosociologist… He thinks that not all your previous personality has gone, that it is still there, latent inside you, or at least part of it is, and that it can merge with your new thought patterns… He is naïve, led astray by his wishes, by his hopes… Oh, Isanusi, can't you see that each person is a unique whole? That there can be no merging of human thought and that of a machine?"

He paused, listening to the empty air, as if he could hear something. Gema asked.

"Thondup, what can I do to...?"

He did not let her finish, but began exclaiming excitedly, "As a cybernetics specialist, I like computers. But in their own place: them there, we humans here..."

"His delirium is getting worse; he thinks he's talking to Isanusi. This can't wait any longer." Gema stood up and went out into the corridor, while Thondup kep talking to someone who wasn't there.

"And don't compare me to those imperial racists; I know full well that all men are equal, yes, but cyberbrains aren't..."

His voice faded to nothing as Gema advanced along the corridor. "I'll have to put him to bed afterwards... otherwise I won't be able to manage him. I'll have to take advantage of his first period of stabilization." She entered the sick bay. "Although there's always... What's going on here?"

Isanusi's sweat-covered face was contracting uncontrollably... "Strengthen the anesthetic." She speeded up. Taking an injector out of the cupboard, she almost ran across to the pod. She searched for a vein and applied the dose... She had to lean on the pod to keep her balance. "Now for Thondup's psychostabilizer; get a move on..." and yet she stood next to the pod until Isanusi's face grew calmer. Only then did she start to look for another injector.

Friday December 31, 2038
11:37 hours

Gema switched off the intercom: "Why is there no reply?"

Leaning back in her seat, she considered this new problem. "He's not visible on the videophones... Yes, he must be in the bathroom in his cabin." She got up and walked to the door. "Is he delirious again? That's unlikely; he would be talking out loud, and I would have heard him..." She left the sick bay and turned right towards the sleeping area. "Perhaps he fainted?" The diagram of the symptoms of radiation sickness came into her mind. She studied it closely. "No, that's almost impossible in this phase." She entered his cabin and strode across to the bathroom door. She knocked loudly.

"Thondup, are you in there?"

No reply. She tried the handle: "It's not locked." She opened it and looked around: "Empty." For a few minutes she stood there without moving, thinking it over. "The last time I saw him was in the lab." She retraced her steps out into the corridor, then headed for the work area. "An accident?" She quickened her pace still further. "It can't have been an explosion; the traces would be on the videophone. Possibly an electrical discharge... But that would have affected the lighting; Palas is not here to compensate for any sudden surges in power..." She went into the lab and looked around. "He was working at that table." As she walked around it, she found Thondup sitting on the floor.

"Why didn't you reply? I've been..."

She fell silent, scrutinized his expressionless face, his empty eyes... She knelt beside him.

"Thondup?"

He gave no sign of having heard her.

Gema thrust her hand into the front pocket of Thondup's spacesuit and pulled out a penlight. She pointed it at his eyes, flashing it on and off. His pupils contracted... "He is still responding."

She continued flashing the light, repeating out loud:

"I'm here, Thondup... Come back... Come on... Thondup..."

A few moments later, he finally blinked. He twisted his head to try to escape the beam of light. Gema slapped his face.

"Wake up now, you're back with us, don't drift away again."

Thondup raised his hand in a clumsy sign of recognition. He murmured:

"Thank you, Gema."

She sat beside him, breathing heavily.

"That was hard work, Thondup. I don't think you should go into any more self-induced hypnotic trances."

"Don't worry, after this experience I prefer the hallucinations."

Gema's eyes lit up with an inquisitive gleam.

"What hallucinations?"

Thondup rubbed the back of his neck energetically.

"From the first day I've been seeing or hearing... some of the dead." He took a deep breath and continued: "This time it was Pavel. I was repairing the receiver and needed a part. I raised my eyes looking for it, and saw him. I asked him to bring it. He didn't move, he just stood there, gazing at me thoughtfully... Annoyed, I stood up to get it myself, and then I remembered. I turned towards him, but he was no longer there. That was when I put myself in a hypnotic trance, so as not to see any repeat of this new vision... And I lost myself."

"Alright, Thondup. If you have another vision, tell me; there's plenty of psychostabilizer left... But now come and eat."

Thondup grimaced.

"I still have no appetite, Gema."

"Are you as thirsty as before?"

"Yes... Not as bad as yesterday, but it's not back to normal yet."

Gema got to her feet first and helped him up.

"Lean on me... that's right."

They left the lab and walked along the corridor. As they passed by the sick bay, Thondup peered inside... He asked, "How is he doing?"

"Not very well."

They went into the restroom and sat down. Thondup smiled weakly:

"Okay, show me the surprise you promised me..."

"Pick up the hydrophore and drink as much as you can."

"Gema, if I fill myself with water I'm sure I won't be able to eat, however appetizing your surprise is."

"Drink and you'll see."

Thondup stared at her for a moment, intrigued. Then he picked up the hydrophore, took a sip... He removed the tube from his mouth.

"This isn't water, Gema."

"Does it taste good?"

Thondup drank again, more deeply this time.

"Yes, it's not bad."

More relaxed, Gema leaned back in her seat. She sighed:

"So that problem's solved at least. If only..."

Instinctively, she reached out to clutch the arms of the chair and managed to resist the force trying to pluck her out of it. Once the acceleration had finished, Thondup murmured:

"Another change of course?"

"Yes. I have to go. The sooner I change the trajectory the better..."

"That's the third time today, isn't it?"

Gema was already on her feet. She nodded without speaking.

"And we're still a long way from the asteroid belt and outside the plane of maximum density... Will we have enough fuel, Gema?"

Nobody answered. Thondup looked around him; she had already left the room. Shrugging his shoulders, he picked up the hydrophore again and drank some more.

"No, it's not bad at all."

14:52 hours

"Seventeen, eighteen, nineteen…" Then the number fifteen appeared at the end of the series flashing on the screen, almost immediately followed by sixteen. Gema let go of Isanusi's hand. "His pulse is quickening; he must be about to wake up." She called out softly:

"Isanusi…"

The eyelids of the man stretched out inside the pod flickered, and Isanusi asked:

"What do you want, Gema…? Has the treatment finished?"

"Yes."

"Well? Has it worked?"

"More or less. The destruction of the nerves is not as rapid as before, but it hasn't stopped completely."

It took Isanusi some time to respond.

"And how are you two?"

"Better."

"More details please, Gema."

"The nausea, vomiting, and diarrhea have stopped. Although we are still weak, it has eased up. We can work without so many interruptions."

"Good. And Thondup's behavior?"

"Acceptable."

"He hasn't had any more crises?"

"He was slightly delirious last night; now he is normal."

"So you'll get better?"

"Too soon to tell. I need to see how our physiological state evolves."

"Yes… What do the blood tests show?"

"Normal, up to now. But any changes will only appear after the third day, so that doesn't mean much."

"Yes, I see…"

"Isanusi, I'm going to try a fresh solution on you. Do you agree?"

"Wait a while. Did Thondup explain the conditioning to you?"

"Yes."

"Was it helpful?"

"Reasonably. Why didn't they include all that explanation in my memory? I wouldn't have had to waste so much time…"

"Can you undertake the task now?"

"Which task?"

"Rescue all you can from your previous mental make-up, and merge it with your new one. Do you think you can do that?"

"There's a good probability of it, but… I'm overwhelmed with work. And to do what you're suggesting takes time. I don't know if I'll have enough to recover what you want before it finally disappears."

"You're not saying what you really think, Gema."

The young woman said nothing.

"Speak."

"Isanusi… Thondup is a psychosociologist."

"I know, he has been for a long time."

"He doesn't think it's possible."

"There's no reason he has to be right; there's no precedent for this kind of conditioning, Gema. Everything we say to you is simply speculation… The result depends on you, on your efforts."

"Alright…" She waited. "Don't you have anything more to add?"

"No."

"Until tomorrow then."

23:49 hours

Thondup shifted restlessly in the bed for the umpteenth time, and Gema asked him:

"Aren't you sleepy?"

"No…" He sat up and looked down at Gema's motionless body. Her unblinking eyes were wide open. He inquired;

"What about you, can you still not sleep?"

"No."

"Didn't you sleep last night either?"

"No, I didn't."

Thondup breathed heavily.

"This wasn't foreseen… and yet it was to be expected."

Gema turned towards him, her curiosity aroused.

"Why? Can you explain it?"

"Yes. Sleep was never included in Proteus' central program…" He scanned Gema's calm face. "Although, in fact, I don't know how you do it. I suppose you're never completely awake, but that the parts of your brain you're not using now are sleeping, or are involved in some sort of similar process. Later it will be the turn of those parts that are awake now, while those now resting come into play… It's a shame I can't study your encephalograms. Is there no chance of doing one?"

"Not without the diagnoser. Not with the precision you'd need…"

Thondup grunted and stretched out again in the bed. After a while, Gema took up the conversation:

"And why can't you sleep?"

"I'm thinking that this is the last night of the year… Alix and I were preparing a few surprises for you, Isanusi, for Pavel and Kay…"

Gema waited for him to go on, but that was all he said. She felt discouraged:

"He's still incomprehensible." She suggested: "Would you like a sleeping pill, Thondup?"

He gave this some thought, before replying:

"No." He got up from the bed and started getting dressed. "I'd better make a start on repairing the receiver. I think I've found the key to make it work again…"

"I'll go with you. Perhaps I can help. I'm tired of thinking so much."

"No." Then Thondup thought better of it and changed his mind.

"Alright, come with me."

He waited for her to get dressed, closely watching all her movements. "It's Gema's body, but it's not her way of moving… Although there is a slight similarity. Her reflex actions are the same. But it's definitely not her." Gema fastened the last clasp and went over to him, smiling.

"Shall we go?"

"Yes, let's go."

They went out into the corridor. Thondup let her go first. He stared at her back as they walked. "Yes, she smiled at me. Almost, almost like before… Is that another reflex?"

Gema realized he was no longer following her. Looking over her shoulder, she saw he was leaning against the wall, deep in thought.

"Did you forget something?"

Thondup looked up sharply.

"No, I was just thinking… I'm coming."

He walked up to her, eyes on the floor. Gema allowed her smile to fade. "He didn't respond to my smile with one of his own, like he used to… Didn't I do it properly?" She walked on, her expression troubled. "It's not that easy, Isanusi, it isn't…"

Saturday January 1, 2039
07:11 hours

Thondup looked away from the phosphorescent dial on the wall, and stretched pleasurably. "It's early yet." Turning on his side, he surveyed Alix. She was lying on her back, her short golden hair lying in untidy curls around her face... His breathing came more quickly; he smiled. "There's still time, I could..." He reached out a hand to gently caress her breasts. He noticed the dark nipples hardening, becoming erect. He snuggled closer, whispering:

"Alix... my love..."

Then from Alix's mouth came Gema's voice:

"Are you hallucinating again, Thondup?"

He froze. To his astonishment, he saw Alix's hair grow longer, darker. Her face grew thinner, with sharper features, turning into Gema's... Shaking her long black locks, she answered her own question:

"I can see from your reaction that I guessed right... Do you need a psychostabilizer?"

Moistening his lips, Thondup shook his head.

"Fine..." Gema gazed inquisitively at the immobile man. She suggested: "I don't mind if you want to carry on. I think you've recovered sufficiently... Yes, perhaps you need to..."

Thondup regained his voice.

"No!" he cried. Jumping out of the bed, he ran to the bathroom.

Gema examined her body with interest. "Interesting... It's similar, and yet not the same as before. Possibly it would be good to carry on; it would be a good reference point..." She turned her gaze to the closed bathroom door. She frowned. "It looks as if that's going to be impossible. I'd better concentrate on the problems while Thondup is getting ready." She reflected for some time, before realizing that Thondup was taking too long. She stood up and went over to the bathroom door.

She asked, "Will you be long?"

Silence.

"Thondup, is something wrong?" She shook the lock on the door; it was turned. "Answer me!"

A dull murmur came from the far side:

"No, nothing."

"Alright."

She waited. "I ought to go and see how Isanusi is getting on. I can't afford to waste any more time."

"Thondup, I'm going to the other bathroom, alright?"

A grunt of assent.

"I'll expect you at nine o'clock for the blood test. Don't forget."

Another grunt. Gema picked up her spacesuit and went back to her former cabin.

13:16 hours

The lisosol appeared, forming a small blue-tinged cloud, then fell gently, slowly... Inside the bone, the molecules sought each other out, then merged, creating a transparent film that covered the tiny blood clots. Dissatisfied, Gema pressed the atomizer again... Isanusi's lips quivered. "He's waking up; I finished in time."

"Who's there? Is that you, Gema?"

"Yes. It's me."

"Good... How did the new treatment go?"

"The same as the first one... Can't you feel anything, Isanusi?"

Gema waited for his reply, plucking at her lower lip.

"Yes, as if someone were pressing on my eyes. It's not exactly painful..."

"Yes, that was to be expected; a phantom sensation."

"What do you mean?"

"The destruction has continued, Isanusi. It was already well-advanced in the optic nerves; another ten millimeters and it would have reached the brain... If I had waited for that, I wouldn't have been able to do anything."

"So you..."

Even though Isanusi could not see her, Gema nodded.

"Yes, I had to enucleate your eyes."

20:00 hours

The pincer trembled slightly... Thondup pressed down on his elbow, waiting for the tiny vibration to cease. His head was still tilted to one side to prevent his breath from reaching the interior of the receiver. A precise movement, and the circuit was reestablished.

Behind Thondup's back, Gema let out her breath. While Thondup replaced the cover, she asked, "Have you fixed it?"

"Yes."

"Can I tell Isanusi?"

Thondup straightened in his seat and wiped the sweat from his brow. He said,

"There are still some things I need to check... But I think you can tell him."

Gema hastily went over to the videophone and switched it on. Isanusi appeared on the screen, his body prone in the pod.

"Isanusi, the receiver is almost ready; we can watch at least some of the transmission tonight. Stay alert: I'm going to leave the intercom on."

20:06 hours

A million harps began to play, soaring, soaring, trying to reach, to surpass infinity… but failed; all too soon, the final notes lapsed into silence.

"Has it broken again?" Tensing, Isanusi strained to hear more clearly. He could even make out the dim flow of blood through his veins… Mingling with that, a gentle murmur began to grow. It gradually swelled into a rushing river flowing towards the unknown, dragging Isanusi with it… Voices that were more human sobbed their happiness; they tirelessly played and replayed the same six notes, each time discovering new possibilities for astonishment, emotion, love… Then the non-human voices returned, overlaying the others, wordlessly telling of something incredibly beautiful, relieving the anxiety to hear those six notes, taking Isanusi to an ever-changing rainbow sky; he ran, shouting with the ardent voices and weeping when they moved on, seeking out other skies…

"I'm sorry, Isanusi; but you mustn't carry on listening."

Gema's voice faded away, and the silver bells fell silent. The lining of the pod wrinkled, rising to his empty eye-sockets, soaking up the pools of tears.

It was only then that Gema switched off the visual channel and returned alongside Thondup. She glanced at his red face… "No, it's not doing him any good either. But I can't get involved."

Seated next to each other, they listened until the music ended. After a brief interval, they heard the familiar voice from Earth:

"You have been listening to the second movement of the Stellar Pathway, the winner of this year's Musical Olympics. Its composer will be no stranger to many of you, especially for the most recent cosmogroups. It is the former 18-L group, now called the Beethoven group. As you will have appreciated, they thoroughly deserve their new name... And now, a report on the first interstellar probe. Over to you, Vera."

A slight cough, and a warm female voice began:

"Yesterday I visited the Project Center... There I was shown a scale model of the automatic exploratory probe that will head for Tau Ceti this year. They dismantled it, kindly explaining to me at every stage how each part worked. I have to admit I did not understand everything, possibly because I was being shown the most recent advances in astronautics, which are often obscure for non-experts. Possibly also because I was thinking of something else... which I feel I ought to tell you about. I cannot deny that great interest has been shown in this probe here on Earth. I think you will understand the kind of interest I mean: a glance at the news, a smile of approval, a comment to friends, and then immersing oneself again in our daily tasks... I fear that here on Earth we have not properly assimilated the real magnitude of this new step towards the Cosmos. Perhaps we have grown accustomed too quickly to the Universe you have opened up for us and continue to amplify... Perhaps we have shut ourselves up too much in our own Earth. What real significance do a few thousand men and women have, dispersed among a dozen bases between Venus and Jupiter? None of those planets can compare with Earth. In truth, for many years to come, possibly forever, we will be distant, alien to them... There is only one Earth in the solar system, and there is nothing more beautiful. So what drives us to go beyond it?"

The voice laughed softly. "I'm sorry; I was forgetting that I am talking to people who know the answer to that question. Not only do they know it, but they feel it inside themselves to such an extent that they have devoted their lives to it, however distant the goal ... To you then it is enough to say it is highly likely that there is a planetary system in Tau Ceti and another in Altair; that the discovery of hydrogen in its hyper-dense state has led to the construction of spaceships that will attain speeds close to the speed of light, and you will start to dream ... That's not a reproach; dreams such as yours have taken humanity further and further, but unfortunately these first new craft will not be able to carry human crews ... No, you will not be going to Tau or to Altair. The information these probes send back will take, respectively, no less than twenty-five and forty years to arrive here ... And yet I know you will continue to dream. And you will continue to work to make your dream, our dream, a reality, so that others, who will not be you, can head for the Earths awaiting us in this vast Universe ...

Yes, that is the future. Yes, it is a long way from being the present; for now, you will continue to live on the bases in space, far from the Earth you long for so much ... You will continue working to provide humanity with new dwelling places. And for all this I can only say one word: Thanks."

The receiver emitted a strange sound, similar to a sob. Gema cast Thondup a sideways glance. "Unsuitable; that's the best description for such a broadcast."

The announcer's voice came on, sounding forced:

"And now, a report on the state of negotiations between the World Communist Federation and the Empire, presented by..."

The announcer broke off suddenly: instinctively, Thondup's hand moved towards the controls... But before he could begin to check them, the announcer's voice returned, this time with an anxious edge to it:

"We beg our listeners to excuse us a moment..."

He fell silent again. Thondup and Gema waited:

"...To return to our transmission; we have just received official confirmation that the entire Cosmic Council has presented their resignation. The Supreme Council of the Federation has accepted this, on condition that they remain in their posts until the next Assembly, due to take place in March, when their successors will be appointed... The Cosmic Council has asked, and the Supreme Council agreed, for the following announcement to be broadcast to the whole Solar System..."

There followed a pause, with the sound of rustling papers:

"We, the members of the Cosmic Council, accept full responsibility for everything that has happened to the Titan Group on its return to Earth."

Thondup and Gema exchanged rapid glances. The announcer went on, in a voice struggling to stay calm:

"Unfortunately, time does not permit us to broadcast the promised report on the negotiations between the Federation and the Empire ... We will renew our attempts to reestablish communication with the spaceship *Sviatagor*; in order to do so, we would ask you to close down all your receivers."

Gema's eyes narrowed. "Why are they ordering them to get off the air? What can they have to say to us they don't want anyone else to hear...?" A glimmer of comprehension flashed through her mind. She leapt towards the receiver, which was shrieking:

"Earth to *Sviatagor*..."

A fraction of a second before Gema could finish turning down the sound the equipment fell silent. "Too late." Thondup was already beside her. He took her hand off the regulator and began to increase the volume with exaggerated care. The receiver was still mute. Thondup's lips began visibly to tremble.

Gema said, "It's useless feeling sorry for ourselves, Thondup."

He gave no indication of having heard her. A bemused expression on his face, he wondered out loud:

"Why didn't I think of that before? It was what was most likely to happen, if the spaceship wasn't completely destroyed... Damage to the system for amplifying audio signals; that's what they must have thought back on Earth..."

"Thondup!"

He looked blankly towards Gema. Stressing each syllable, she asked him,

"Can you fix it?"

Thondup looked doubtful as he gazed at the apparatus.

"As long as it's not the audio relay again... That was the last spare part I had..."

Gema turned and, without looking back, headed for her workbench in search of a psychostabilizer.

22:31 hours

Two bodies stretched out on a bed. Two pairs of eyes staring at the ceiling... Gema's head turned towards the man:

"Why aren't you sleeping, Thondup?"

He sighed.

"I was remembering the 18-L group... They were in their last year when we reached the Academy. Do you remember Anke? Always so cheerful, so caring. Do you remember how she became our friend, even though we were no more than kids, freshly arrived and with no experience... I've forgotten why they didn't go on..."

"Liu suffered from cosmic vertigo. It was discovered during her stay in the Orbital City."

"See? An illness that affects one in every ten thousand; and for one of us to get it... a real shame; it was a good group."

"Kriegman's physiological collective is developing a promising new procedure..."

Thondup shifted his shoulders impatiently.

"That will be too late for them, Gema..." His voice became dreamy once more.

"I can almost see them now, on the day when they learned they would not be able to... All eight of them were sitting together on the Pioneer Promenade, staring at the monuments. Some others would come up, sit with them for a while, also in silence... and then walk on. They themselves left when it was evening... Anke saw me; I hadn't dared approach them. She smiled, so I went up to her. That was when she told me she had decided to dedicate herself to emotional engineering. I'm really pleased they succeeded; it's a well-deserved reward."

Gema hesitated a few moments before deciding to speak:

"Thondup, forgive me if I'm asking you something obvious, but I'm trying to understand better... Do you think Anke is happy now?"

Taken aback, Thondup looked across at Gema.

"It seems to me I didn't get your question."

Gema tried to explain:

"I'm asking whether you think the success they've achieved has really compensated her for not... for not having reached here." She swept her arm around the cabin. Thondup thought it over for a long while. Gema waited patiently for his reply.

"No."

They both fell silent again.

23:25 hours

Thondup tautened his neck muscles and raised his head.

"Your arm must be numb, Gema."

She tensed it, stretched out her fingers.

"It's not too bad... But if you like, come closer to me."

Thondup relaxed his head again, this time on Gema's shoulder. She passed her arm around his neck until her hand rested on his chest. She ordered him:

"Now go to sleep. You need it."

Thondup looked up at Gema's dark eyes, and asked,

"Why are you keeping Isanusi alive?"

"Isn't that what I should be doing?"

Deep furrows appeared at the corners of Thondup's mouth.

"He's suffering, Gema."

"He can't feel pain; his nerve sensors are all dead."

"But he understands. There are other things beside physical pain. He suffers to see himself as an invalid, as simply another burden, knowing he is bound to die anyway... He also suffers at seeing us in this situation and being unable to do anything to help." He sat up in the bed, facing Gema. "You cannot comprehend this, but in reality what we are doing is torturing him."

Gema also sat up slowly. Her voice was flat, expressionless:

"I have my own view of that, Thondup. You and I are the invalids;

his is the only mind that has remained unchanged, that still operates and is human. He is the only one I can really trust... I'm sorry, but I had to tell you. I know it's not your fault that you are in this situation... Once we've got all the necessary elements to make a decision, we will need Isanusi. What is more, he knows it; if he himself had thought he was a burden to us, he would have asked to us put him to death by now... And I must tell you that this opinion does not come solely from what I am now; as far as I can recollect, the former Gema would have thought the same."

She waited for Thondup to respond.

He stretched out again, and Gema did likewise, staring at his back. She whispered,

"Don't think it's because I dislike you, Thondup... Remember, I cannot feel such emotions. Come closer."

Thondup's head was soon nestling on her shoulder once more.

Sunday January 2, 2039
00:12 hours

The door to the cabin opened silently, and Gema entered. Thondup asked from the bed:

"Have you corrected the trajectory?"

Half-undressed by now, Gema nodded, then inquired:

"What about you, still not sleepy?"

"No."

Gema disappeared into the bathroom. Thondup went on:

"What a shame they couldn't transmit the report on the negotiations between the Empire and the Federation... What do you think, Gema? Do you think anything will come of it this time?"

She came out of the bathroom with a glass of water in one hand and a grey pill in the other. She replied:

"Yes. Here, take this."

Thondup surveyed her curiously... Straightening up in the bed, he took the pill and began rolling it around in his hand.

"So you think that... And have you also been able to work out what the result will be?"

"Naturally. The Empire will dissolve, and the countries that made it up will become part of the Federation." She held out the glass, and said, "Make sure you take it, Thondup."

He swallowed the pill and drank the water. He answered:

"I don't see how the imperial clique would agree to renounce all their privileges... What are you basing your judgment on, Gema?"

By now she was already in bed. Turning towards her, Thondup regarded her with a mixture of curiosity and doubt. Gema replied,

"The key factor: the Dream Palaces."

Thondup's voice reflected his skepticism.

"Is that all? But Gema, the imperial government itself has prohibited new construction... So what influence can they have?"

The young woman sighed.

"I can see I'll have to start from the very beginning... Thondup, for various reasons I have had to study the human way of thinking, even that of the Empire, from my current perspective. Listen: the capitalist mentality is based on the cult of individualism, the supremacy of the self over the others, over all of society, isn't that so?"

"Yes, that's elementary... But what has that got to do with what we are talking about?"

"Be patient. For an individual who is contemptuous of society, who sees it as his enemy and only values his own interests, what is his basic need, his highest aspiration?"

Thondup shrugged.

"That's elementary too: his own pleasure."

Gema nodded.

"So, from that point of view, look at the facts..."

Thondup's mouth widened in a yawn he could not suppress. "The sleeping pill is taking effect," Gema realized. An idea came into her mind: "Why not try now? His critical faculties must have lessened... Perhaps he won't realize I am speaking just like the old Gema."

Without any perceptible pause, she continued, with only a slight change in her tone of voice:

"...The first imperial Dream Palace is being built: Who can pay for a century of living, beautiful dreams? The answer is obvious, Thondup. And the choice of the Dream is understandable too, from their point of view. Thanks to it, there is no danger of any frustration, of experiencing the failures threatening them in this so unpleasantly real world of ours. Yes, in the Dream they will also come up against adversaries envious of their riches and power, but they are there solely in order that the dreamer may experience the pleasure of crushing them... In the Dream world they can do whatever they wish, without restrictions, without any real opposition. Now put yourself in the place of the imperial leaders. What are they likely to choose between a dream and an increasingly harsh reality?"

Thondup managed to raise his eyelids and answer in a sleepy voice:

"Yes, there's a logic to that, and yet in the end, a dream is not reality..." He yawned once more, before concluding: "That's why it could never satisfy them, Gema."

"It seems to me you haven't taken your analysis of the individualistic way of behaving to its ultimate consequences... Don't you remember solipsism, Thondup?" He nodded, but Gema could not tell if this was in agreement or simply that he was falling asleep. "That is the logical consequence of a thought process focused entirely on the self: "What my senses perceive is real. If what reaches me from the outside, from the Non-Self is the Dream, then that is what reality is." That must be what the members of the imperial elite think and feel. Possibly now you'll understand what has been going on in recent years. One after another, their leaders have yielded to a curiosity to know what the Dream is, and have all tried it. Ever since, all they desire is to live in their Dream… The process is unstoppable; one after another, they have sought refuge in the Dream Palaces that have sprung up all over the place. Those people have been replaced, but the new ones are unable to resist the temptation either… Do you understand now why the imperial leaders last for such a short time, why they suddenly vanish? They are there, in their Dreams. Yes, so now it is strictly forbidden to construct any new Dream Palaces; the successors of the successors have become aware of the progressive weakening of the ruling class and have reflected on all this…"

His voice slurred, Thondup interrupted her:

"Doesn't that mean that the Dream Palaces are no longer a danger to the Empire, Gema?"

"That's an error of judgment, Thondup. Do you think they haven't experimented with the Dream as well? That somehow they don't want to seek refuge there too and no longer be the guard-dogs for all those already dreaming, those who already possess the happiness they themselves long for? Why cling to this world and its tottering Empire? Why go on facing real difficulties and dangers when there's a niche waiting for them in one of the Dream Palaces? Isn't it better for them to do a deal? To say, 'You respect our Dreams, and we will no longer stand in the way of History?' There's no doubt that is their safest option. They can see that the Empire is drawing perilously close to its final crisis, which means anything can happen. The Dream Palaces are shielded against the direct effects of an atomic war, but their energy sources aren't. The fear that they could wake from their artificial paradise and find themselves in a devastated world was and is the best possible argument. For the first time ever, their egoism and the needs of humanity coincide..."

Gema stopped. She settled the sleeping Thondup in the bed, and stretched out beside him. "I don't think I did that any worse than the old Gema... We can continue tomorrow."

09:01 hours

The drop of blood fell; an instant later, sections of the slender, transparent capillaries turned red where the luminous beams crossed them... At the far end, opposite the optical lasers, microscopic shadows formed; photoelements measured, classified, and counted them time and again until the margin of error became negligible. Then the figures flashed on the screen of the microanalyzer in rapid succession, only to vanish almost as quickly—though not before they were recorded on Gema's mind. Similar figures from the preceding days emerged from the depths of her memory. Gema automatically compared them,

"Red cells, normal; leucocytes, a small but insignificant drop... platelets, a pronounced fall." she shook her head. "It seems as though Thondup was the worst affected." Without turning around, she instructed:

"Take your clothes off, Thondup."

He looked up from the red pinprick on his finger and asked, puzzled, "Why is that, Gema?"

"Don't think it's because I want to admire your body; I need to examine your skin."

Thondup reluctantly began to take off his suit.

"But Gema, our morning inspection isn't finished yet…"

"I won't be long." She turned towards him, a smile on her face. "Lie down here… on your back, please."

"At your service…"

Thondup settled in the pod. Gema leaned over him, surveying every inch of his body. The smile disappeared.

"Thondup, look here." She pointed at his side. "Have you seen this petechia before?"

Craning his neck, Thondup looked down. He shook his head.

"No, I don't recall ever having seen that before. What has caused it?"

"A weakness in your capillaries."

"And what does it mean, this petechia or whatever it's called?"

Gema tried to smile reassuringly.

"You got the name right, it's a petechia… and it means we need to avoid any blow or cut. They could produce a hemorrhage that would be hard to stem." She finished her examination while she was speaking. Straightening up with a sigh, she commented, "I can't see anything more here; turn on your front."

Thondup obeyed, and Gema again brought her face close to his golden skin… Soon afterwards, she straightened again:

"No, you don't have any others. Now you have to examine me; look for anything similar to your petechia."

Thondup got up from the pod and put his suit on; Gema did the opposite. He bent over the female body lying on her front, surveying it closely… All of a sudden, Gema spoke:

"We'll have to take fresh precautions, Thondup."

"What against?"

"Against falls or stumbles caused by uncoordinated movements…"

"But it was only on the first day that we had problems with our motor functions, Gema. Now I at least can move freely."

"The problems will be back, Thondup."

Thondup frowned.

"So things don't look good?"

"Don't be in such a hurry; I still don't have enough data to be able to make a firm diagnosis."

"Fine… But tell me what concrete measures you're proposing."

"To use polyfoam to cover the floor, the walls, any sharp edge, wherever it may be."

Thondup straightened up, hands akimbo.

"This is tiring… Nothing on your back, you can turn around. Do we have enough polyfoam left?"

"If we are careful with it, yes."

Thondup leaned closer to the young woman, narrowing his eyes:

"Look at this, Gema."

She raised her head to look at the tip of her left breast that Thondup was pointing to but immediately fell back.

"No, Thondup; that's a birth mark, not a lesion, you ought to know."

Thondup blew out his cheeks.

"Remember I'm not a physiologist like you. Perhaps if I were Isanusi, I would have paid attention to it."

The gleam in Gema's eyes had something of her old sense of humor:

"Well, in the end you're not doing too badly… Knowing how observant you usually are, I was worried at first you might think my nipple was a melanoma."

Thondup smiled despite himself.

"Thanks for the praise… But to be serious once more, aren't these petachiae a bad sign?"

"They may or may not be... Don't tickle me."

"Put up with it... I did."

Thondup took a step to the left and concentrated his attention on Gema's legs.

"What's this?"

"Where?"

"On the outside of your right thigh. It looks more like a bruise."

"Yes, it is. It's a souvenir of the day of the accident. Carry on."

"Let's see... No, nothing else. You can get dressed, dear patient."

Gema jumped nimbly out of the pod and took the spacesuit that Thondup was gallantly holding out. She gave him a broad smile of thanks. "He reacts favorably to the new code of conduct. New? No, the old one... I think I can suspend the psychostabilizers, he seems to have stabilized." Doing up the last clasp, she asked:

"When shall we spread the polyfoam?"

"Can we leave it until this afternoon? Don't forget I have to finish the inspection."

"Alright, this afternoon."

Thondup left the lab. Gema's face lost all expression. She went over to the intercom's blank screen:

"What do you think, Isanusi?"

A hoarse whisper came from the machine:

"What do you mean?"

"My conduct, of course. I think I did a good imitation of the old Gema; Thondup behaved as though nothing had happened... didn't he?" Slightly anxious, she also switched on the visual channel, and studied the face of the man lying in the recovery pod in the sick bay. She added hesitantly, "Didn't he behave like he used to?"

"Don't worry; yes, he behaved just like before... It's something else that worries me. I don't think you understood me, Gema: I didn't ask you to copy your former personality but to integrate the elements you could rescue into your present mental make-up..."

"I'm trying to do that, Isanusi, but don't imagine it's easy. To be honest, I still haven't really understood... I think that being able to imitate Gema's attitudes and reactions in a way that Thondup finds convincing is a great success."

Isanusi took some time to reply.

"Yes, possibly you're right... You're in the best position to judge how hard your task is. But don't be satisfied with just mastering appearances: you need to reach the essence. Thondup may not have noticed that, but I did."

"I'll work on capturing the essence as well, Isanusi."

"Not capturing it..."

"Yes, I understand: integrating it."

Isanusi's eyebrows fell almost as far as his empty eye-sockets, in a gesture of agreement.

15:47 hours

Gema paused and wiped the sweat from her brow. "Thankfully there's not a lot more to do." Looking across at Thondup, her eyes opened wide: "What's he doing?" The thin jet of polyfoam was being sprayed here and there, making grey patterns:

"This isn't a game, Thondup."

The spray went on dancing in the man's hands. He replied over his shoulder:

"Gema, don't be so... efficient."

Going over to him, she stretched out her hand:

"I can see you're tired. Give it to me. I'll finish on my own."

Thondup cast her a sideways glance.

"No."

"Thondup, there isn't going to be enough..."

"There will be."

Disconcerted, Gema did not move. "What shall I do?" She examined his face. "He looks normal, but..."

The screech of the alarm reached her. "Isanusi!" She ran as fast as she could along the corridor. "Did the alarm go off in time?" She pushed open the sick bay door and rushed in. Reaching the recovery pod, she read the indications on the screens... "His lungs... hurry!" Her hands ran over the control panel, pressing here, turning a button there. She stopped to look... the lid rose, covering Isanusi's upper body. The new skin contracted, expanded, then contracted again, over and over again as Gema tensely observed the immobile face... Some time later, the prone man's lips quivered.

"Isanusi?"

An inarticulate sigh came from inside the pod.

"Isanusi, if you want to say something, take advantage of the moment the air leaves your lungs."

"Is that..." the cover bulged, then started to contract again... "is that you, Gema?"

She smiled and hastily replied:

"Yes, it's me. Do you feel alright?"

"Yes... I had... a bad moment, that's all... but it's passed now."

Gema's hand brushed Isanusi's face. She advised him:

"Don't force yourself to speak; it's better if you rest..." She remembered something and frowned. "I have to go now, there's something I need to do... I'll be back as soon as possible."

15:53 hours

"Thondup, what are you doing?"

He did not reply, but simply stood there, legs apart, a dreamy look on his face. Gema saw he had left his boots over by the wall.

"Why are you barefoot?"

Slowly, Thondup raised one foot from the layer of polyfoam and stared down at it, wiggling his toes. The imprint his foot had left slowly faded... He beamed at Gema and said:

"Ever since I was a boy, I've dreamed of walking on clouds." He smiled. "Go on, you try it too."

She hesitated, but only for a second, then took off her boots.

"Yes, it's nice, really nice. You're right, Thondup, it's better to go around barefoot." She saw his smile grow even broader.

"I was right; it can't be hard to manipulate him." Smiling back at him, she went on:

"We should walk a bit to feel it more. Come on, let's go to the lab."

His eyes narrowed suspiciously.

"Why?"

"Have you forgotten already? We agreed yesterday we would have two blood tests each day. One in the morning, and the other in the afternoon..."

A glint of acknowledgment appeared in his eyes. He nodded.

"Yes, I remember..."

Gema took him by the arm. "First the blood test; then the psychostabilizer... I'm going to have to give it to him permanently." They walked side by side down the now grey corridor. Gema kept glancing sideways at Thondup's face and noticed it gradually changing..." Oh, no! Not a depressive mood right now!" All at once Thondup stopped and buried his face in his hands.

"What's the matter, Thondup?"

His fingers spread open slightly, revealing his terrified eyes. Gema took a step back.

"What's wrong?"

The man sat heavily down on the floor. Gema went up to him, and could hear him moaning:

"Unbearable... unbearable... unbearable..."

"This isn't getting us anywhere," thought Gema.

"Shut up!" she shouted, and Thondup fell silent. Trying to soften her voice, Gema insisted: "Tell me, what's so unbearable?"

Thondup's left hand moved from his face and pointed at the wall.

Gema surveyed it closely... "I can't see anything there, Thondup."

His other hand dropped, and he stared at her incredulously.

"But can't you see that wall?"

"Of course I can, Thondup, but there's nothing special about it."

"Nothing? Nothing? What about that horrible grey color?"

His face twisted in a grimace.

"Grey, grey, grey, nothing but grey... I can't stand it, Gema; protect me, please..."

He screwed his eyes up tight again.

"Yes, I'll help you, Thondup, but you need to stand up."

He struggled to his feet, his hands groping at the air.

Gema took his arm.

"Come on; follow me."

They walked slowly and in silence to the lab, then Gema directed him to the work bench.

"Sit here... that's right."

She let go of his arm, and Thondup gripped the arms of the chair tightly, his eyes still closed. Gema swiftly connected the microanalyzer, picked up the extractor, and went back to him.

"Give me your hand... No, not like that, open it for me."

The fingers slowly uncurled... She took hold of his first finger and jabbed the slender point of the extractor into his flesh. Thondup shuddered and opened his eyes. He watched as Gema drew out the sample, the drop of blood forming on his fingertip. A smile appeared on his face. Gema hastily emptied the sample from the extractor into the top of the microanalyzer.

"Wait a moment, Thondup..."

The figures flashed up on the screen and quickly disappeared. Red blood cells, normal; leucocytes, no significant reduction. The platelets are continuing to diminish."

She disconnected the microanalyzer and turned to Thondup.

"Now... what are you doing?"

Leaning over the arm of his chair with his face close to the floor, Thondup was squeezing the punctured finger with his other hand. Gema bent over him:

"Does it hurt?"

Thondup smiled up at her.

"Look how beautiful it is, Gema..."

Gema looked: half a dozen bright scarlet drops of blood stood out on the grey polyfoam. While she was contemplating them, another drop fell, then another...

"Yes, it's very pretty... but you do know they'll disappear, don't you?"

The smile vanished from Thondup's face.. Gema insisted:

"Yes, it's not going to last, it'll soon be all grey again." Gema looked for the tube of coagulant on the bench. "Give me your hand..."

A sudden gleam came into Thondup's eyes.

"I know!" He rose triumphantly. "I know!" he repeated.

"What do you know?"

"The sprays!" He ran out into the corridor. Gema searched desperately on the bench for a psychostabilizer. She picked it up, and hesitated for an instant... "In his present state, this won't be enough." She unscrewed the injector, took a capsule of psychodepressant, and inserted it. "That ought to be enough." She walked towards the corridor but stopped in the hatchway. "Where can he have got to?" She looked down at the floor: every few steps she could see fresh, shiny drops of blood. Gema followed them, head down.

Thondup pressed the can in his right hand with all his strength; there was another explosion of color on the wall... A few greenish trails dripped to the floor and stopped. He squeezed the can in his left hand, and a yellow patch appeared alongside the green one.

"Thondup!"

He threw away the empty cans, then searched for some new ones in the bag hanging over his shoulder. He muttered: "Red... we need that, and purple too... White? No, not now. Dark brown?" He thought it over. "Yes, brown would be good... Not black... Blue!" He pulled out both hands, each holding a fresh can. He looked up, and when he saw Gema, he smiled contentedly at her. "Here you are finally." He held the cans out to her. "Here, I've got more," he said, generously offering them. Gema did not move but looked down at his blood-stained right hand.

"Wait... it can't be easy for you to press with that hand, can it?"

A sad shadow flitted across Thondup's face.

"Yes, it's true... The can slips."

"I'll fix it; hold it up for me."

Thondup stretched out his arm. Gema spread the coagulant on the tiny wound, while at the same time, without Thondup noticing, jabbed the hidden injector into the palm of his hand. She could feel his muscles tensing beneath her fingers and quickly apologized:

"I'm sorry, I didn't realize I was still holding the injector..." She spread the coagulant over the new pinprick. "But everything is fine now, see: it's not bleeding." She was studying Thondup's face from corner of her eye and carried on talking: "Now, give me my sprays."

He stared at her with a mixture of surprise and hostility. "How long before it takes effect? I should have injected a vein, even though he would have realized..." She insisted: "Don't you remember? You wanted me to help you paint and offered me two cans. Go on, give them to me." He seemed to remember his promise and handed her two cans.

Gema breathed out: "Thank you."

She pressed the can, and a white cloud appeared on the wall.

She smiled convincingly:

"Look how pretty it is... Your turn now."

Next to the cloud, a blue star appeared.

16:39 hours

Leaning against the lab doorway, Gema pointed to the ceiling:

"Look, there's some grey up there still..."

Thondup peered dubiously up at the ceiling. He nodded, unable to speak. He rummaged around in the bag but could not find another can. He peered inside the bag and staggered, then fell to his knees. His eyes were blinking furiously. Gathering his remaining strength, he managed to say,

"No..." and then collapsed.

Gema rubbed her temples with both hands. "What resistance he has... that dose is not going to be enough. I'll have to put him in a pod..." She surveyed her energy reserves. "They won't last... not even for a little while; I won't be able to manage him. Perhaps if I gave him another shot…" As she moved away from the doorway, her legs gave way under her. Before she could lean on the wall for support, she fell. Tears welled in her eyes. "All my reserves have gone." The sound of the sea grew in her ears. "If the walls would only stay still…" Closing her eyes, she plunged into darkness.

17:02 hours

Thondup's eyelids flickered once, twice… then his eyes opened. It took him some time to focus, to realize where he was. "At the entrance to the lab." He looked around, and his eyes fell on Gema's body sprawled a few paces away. After several useless attempts to stand up, he succeeded in propping himself up on his hands and knees and crawled over to her… As his hand brushed her face, she came to. She looked at him and said in a faint voice:

"We'll have to find more sprays, Thondup."

His face flushed. He sat beside her, crossing his legs.

"I must have given you a hard time, Gema." Seeing the look in her eyes, he nodded. "I'm back to normal now. At least, I think I am…"

Leaning her weight on her arms, Gema tried to get up but fell back. She stubbornly managed to reach a sitting position, facing Thondup.

She said laconically,

"I'm pleased for you"

The further Thondup looked along the corridor, the more his cheeks turned pink with embarrassment… He said guiltily,

"It'll take a lot of work to clean the corridor…"

Gema shook her head.

"We don't have the time or the strength, Thondup." She grinned.

"Besides, I don't see the need. The colors keep it from being monotonous ... And I must say, there was too much grey for my taste."

Thondup snorted. "Don't laugh at me, Gema. It's not funny."

Monday January 2, 2039
10:23 hours

A mass of cables and tubes snaked in and out between the pod and all the apparatus surrounding it, forming an intricate three-dimensional figure that left Isanusi's face barely visible. Thondup looked away from him. "Gema is taking too long." As though summoned by his thought, she appeared on the threshold of the sick bay.

"I'm sorry, but I wanted to check some data ..." She sat at the head of the pod. Peering inside it, she asked,

"Isanusi, are you awake?"

The expedition leader's lips moved noiselessly.

Gema assented:

"We can start then. Let's consider the extent of the problem. According to the information Thondup has supplied me with, apart from the long-distance transmitter and the autopilot, *Sviatagor* is functioning satisfactorily..." She anticipated Thondup's reaction: "Yes, I know there are other damaged systems: the diagnoser, the hypnotron and I don't know how many others. But I'm trying to keep to the elements that are strictly necessary to achieve our stated goal: that is, to make sure *Sviatagor* returns to Earth. Bearing that in mind, I am confident that the protective, propulsion, and directional systems are working reasonably well and that our fuel reserves are adequate. Agreed?"

Thondup gave a slight nod.

"Let's move on to the next point then. The crew: there are three of us left. You don't have to be a physiologist to foresee that Isanusi, in his present condition, will not live longer than two or three days at most… And the radiation has badly affected us two. You, Thondup, are likely to die within a minimum of two weeks, or four at the most. I have slightly longer to live; somewhere between four and six weeks. As far as being able to work is concerned though, I won't reach the fourth week. Now, it will take more than two months for the spaceship to reach Earth… so the problem we are facing is serious. Does anyone have any other general point to make?"

Thondup did not say a word. Gema looked inside the pod once more: Isanusi's lips were not moving. She went on:

"The first option I considered was to increase our speed. But that wouldn't work: above 150 kilometers per second, the radiodetection system becomes unreliable. Besides, the relative speed with which *Sviatagor* would collide with any meteorite would be too great for our magnetic shield, the two layers of the hull, and the densiplama. In other words, increasing the speed of *Sviatagor* simply means hastening its destruction." Gema took a deep breath.

"Now for the second possibility: changing our destination. That's to say, what if we abandon the idea of reaching Earth and aim for the nearest base? Unfortunately, Mars is on the far side of the sun… The only base closer to us than Earth is the one on the Ceres asteroid. If we head for that at top speed in a straight line it would not take us more than three weeks… that is, if we didn't have to cross the asteroid belt at its densest. That would mean reducing our speed and constantly having to change direction, so in practice it would take us the same time as it would to reach Earth. Therefore, that option has to be rejected as well…"

"What if we made a detour around the densest part of the Belt?"

"I calculated that option as well; it would take us seven weeks."

"And if we went around, aiming for the satellites of Jupiter?"

"We would have to slow down, then accelerate again. We wouldn't be able to attain full speed, and would have no reserves left for any change of course... It could take as long as three months to reach them. The third choice..."

"Is this one any use?"

"No, Thondup. As I was saying, the third..."

"Wait; why don't you move on directly to the option that will work, if there is one?"

"There are important reasons for me to set them out in this order, Thondup; just be patient."

"Alright..."

"As I was saying, the third option would be to hibernate for six weeks, so that we will still be alive when the spacecraft comes close to Earth. The first problem with that is the impossibility of rectifying our course after the automatic system changes it to avoid any meteorite. We are coming across them on average three times every twenty-four hours, and as we approach the Belt this will become more frequent still. The cumulative effect of these corrections could mean that when we come out of hibernation we are moving away from Earth, instead of getting closer... We could set the craft so that each change is followed by one in the opposite direction, but that would never compensate completely, because the incidents with meteorites are not at regular intervals. That means we could not guarantee that *Sviatagor* would reach Earth..."

"We could hibernate for a week, Gema; wake up for an hour or two, so that I could check the state of all the equipment. You could adjust our course, then we could hibernate again. Is that possible?"

"It's possible. But I calculate that this option would mean taking more than three months to reach the neighborhood of Earth... And there's another objection: if we did that, the hibernation would not be deep enough. We would spend half the week in the process of going into hibernation, and the other half emerging from it. These are precisely the periods when infectious processes could be most dangerous, due to the additional weakness our immune system would suffer, not to mention the effects of the radiation..."

"The hibernation pods can be sterilized, Gema."

"That sterilization would not affect our usual microbic flora, Thondup; it wasn't designed for that. And it is that normally harmless flora that will become infectious with the disappearance of the defense systems of the organism that keep it harmless. No, Thondup; hibernation isn't a choice either."

He drew his hand across his face and sighed.

"Okay. So tell me the fourth option... And I hope it's the right one."

"The fourth option is to accept the fact that we will not be alive when we have the chance to communicate or to land on any base. That being so, we have simply to keep on an approximate course for Earth as long as we are alive. *Sviatagor* will retain its magnetic shield for another year; fuel sufficient to help it avoid obstacles will last a further six months... In that time span, a year and a half, supposing an intensive search for the craft is launched, there is one chance in ninety they will find the ship before it is destroyed."

"I hope that isn't the option you are proposing, Gema."

"No, that's obvious. But before I outline the fifth possibility, I'd like to ask you if you have thought of any way of resolving this problem that has any chance of succeeding."

Thondup shook his head.

"What about you, Isanusi?"

Gema read "No" on his lips.

"Fine… The fifth option is for Isanusi to take control of *Sviatagor* and pilot it back to Earth."

Thondup peered with astonishment at Gema's face.

"This isn't the moment for jokes, Gema."

"I'm not joking."

"Then you've gone mad; how could he possibly do that?" He swept his arm around the cluster of apparatus around the pod. "Come back to reality, Gema; He can't move, see, or even speak… And on top of that, you said yourself that he won't survive another three days."

"In current conditions; I think I made that clear."

"So how could you change them? I think you're malfunctioning…"

"Thondup, if we still had Palas, what would we do?"

"What's that got to do with anything? We don't have Palas, so that's that."

"I can tell you what we would do: we would give him the task of piloting the craft back to Earth. Isn't that right?"

Thondup's mouth slowly dropped open.

"No, Gema. That's not possible."

"Why not? I've been thinking every night how to do it and haven't been able to find any insurmountable obstacle. Palas' system of nutrient circulation is intact and can be adapted to the needs of Isanusi's brain; it will fit into the container where the central logic circuits are located and can completely take over its functions…"

"Gema, no…"

"It's true that Palas's neurons are not exactly the same as ours, but I don't think the differences are crucial. The rest is a question of training Isanusi, to get him used to his new means of perception of the world, his new ways of performing…"

"Gema…"

"That's why I went through the other options first, Thondup. I wanted you to see clearly that this is the only way out."

"There is no way out, Gema."

"Yes, there is: my fifth option. I haven't found any obstacle to it. Can you two see any?"

"Yes."

"Tell me what it is, and we'll find a way around it."

"As long as the two of us are alive, there'll be no problems; I agree with that. But once we have gone, Isanusi's psychological stability will be affected, and he won't be up to piloting the ship back."

"I don't see why... Based on what, Thondup?"

"On the fact that we constituted a group..." He gestured wearily. "It's too long to explain, Gema. But if you want to confirm what I'm saying, ask Isanusi; he knows."

Gema bent over the pod:

"Is it true what Thondup says, Isanusi?"

His lips moved slowly, and she translated the words out loud:

"Yes..."

Leaning back in her chair again, she said in a neutral tone, "It doesn't matter how long the explanation is. I need that information, Thondup. There must be some way..."

Thondup began to speak in a low voice; there was a look of compassion in his eyes: "It's not your fault, Gema; it's hard to realize how much we need air to breathe until it's lacking... I should have warned you about this before now. I'm sorry you've wasted so much time in the analysis of an option that should have been discarded from the beginning."

"Give me the information, Thondup."

He studied Gema's face intently.

"If that's what you want..."

"I do, Thondup."

He leaned back, staring up at the ceiling, then began:

"In the second half of the last century, mankind left Earth for the first time. He did not go far; at the start it was only near orbit, from where the mother planet could be seen, and return was possible in a matter of minutes. Not a great deal of energy was needed to communicate by videophone with their..."

"I've been in the Orbital City, Thondup. You can skip the details."

"But the details are important, Gema. At that distance, it could be said they had not yet really left Earth. The question that concerns us arose with the first interplanetary expeditions, the flights to Mars and Venus... That was a qualitative leap; the Earth became a small shiny object in the distance, months away. All the crews had to remember it by was what they had on board: holograms, the sensory cabin with its smells of woods and the sea... and the crewmembers themselves. Man is a social animal: each small group of cosmonauts had to find within itself all the elements to create a stable society, or rather, a completely stable one, so that there was nothing that..."

"Thondup, none of this is new to me."

"Let me continue in my own way; besides, we have more than enough time... Yes, you're also aware of the system used to create cosmogroups; hundreds of precosmic candidates scattered throughout the Federation, with tens of thousands of children helping them, while at the same time in Stellar City computers and psychosociologists are at work day and night accumulating, classifying and selecting the information collected hour after hour on each of those candidates until one day a decision is made: this is the group. And from the most remote regions come six, or eight, or a dozen youngsters between fourteen and eighteen years of age. They start living together, astonished at how quickly they get along... They spend five or six years together, until a select few of those groups take flight, their flight. All the computers and psychosociologists (and they are not easy to satisfy) are convinced they constitute such a united, solid collectivity that they will be able to face any challenge... As long as they remain intact.

But there are two sides to every coin, and for this one too; these cosmogroups can survive far from the Earth, far from Mankind, for years. And not simply survive, but work together as efficiently or more so than any terrestrial collective... but this is achieved thanks to an extremely close mutual dependence. Maybe an example from popular folklore will help illustrate my point: the story of an old couple who have lived together for so many years that when one of them dies, the other soon follows them to the grave, despite being in good health... Naturally, in present-day society such phenomena are uncommon; given the development and enrichment of the human personality, it is rare to find two individuals whose characters can blend with one another to this extent.

But the cosmogroups have been selected, amongst other things, from among trillions of possible combinations precisely for their ability to blend mutually in this way. The identification the two old people had with each other pales in comparison to the inter-relation created between the members of a cosmogroup. This is to avoid, in whatever situation that might arise, the appearance of tensions or resentment within the group that could damage its efficiency... and yet it also means that we are laying ourselves open to the fate of the surviving partner. All this is closely studied in each group, Gema, to determine how resistant it is to any loss..."

"Training in psychosimulators..."

"That's one of the methods. But let's look at our case: in our group, the break point for losses is two. That means that a minimum of four members are necessary to guarantee its stability; if only three survive, any normal functioning is impossible."

"But so far we have managed to stay an effective group, Thondup."

"If I hadn't activated your conditioning you wouldn't be in a much better state than I am, Gema, and we would have destroyed the spaceship by now. Or am I mistaken?"

She quickly reviewed his argument:

"Yes, you're right."

"Now, I have to admit that Isanusi has demonstrated he has exceptional stability, although it's not easy to determine what would have happened to him if it had been you and not Alix who had been on the bridge when we hit the meteorite… But in any case, he can never be so exceptional as to be able to listen to us die and still keep his mental equilibrium… No, Gema, your fifth option will not work either."

The young woman glanced down at the pod.

"What about you, Isanusi? Can you see any way around this?"

The stricken man's lips moved furiously. Gema translated:

"He says… that because of my conditioning, I am not governed by your reasoning, and that my brain can be used instead of his… But that won't work, Isanusi. Who is going to operate on me? Who can connect my brain to the autopilot and adjust the terminals correctly? Thondup is not a physiologist. Any other ideas?"

This time, the lips did not move. Gema raised her red-rimmed eyes to Thondup and admitted:

"You're right… but give me some time to think, will you?"

Thondup shrugged.

"As you wish; I have nothing urgent to do."

12:18 hours

"I've got it, Thondup... or at least, I've got an idea that we could work with. You can't condition Isanusi, can you?"

"Of course not, Gema."

"I thought not... but that doesn't matter; I think you could put him in a trance or hypnotize him so that he forgets this conversation and get him to believe that we are in the hibernation pods and that he shouldn't wake us but should..."

"That won't work, Gema; I don't have the means to induce such a state in him. Cases like that need a highly specialized laboratory and a lot of time... Gema!"

"What is it?"

"Couldn't that be the solution? To connect him to the autopilot while we get into the hibernators?"

"No. It would take at least three weeks to teach him, and for us to keep on piloting the ship while he was learning; by then most probably you would be dead, and I would be in no state to survive hibernation; I would die in the process... No, Thondup, give it more thought."

And they gave it more thought.

12:35 hours

"Gema..."

She opened her eyes.

"What is it?"

"I have an idea... an absurd one, of course."

"Don't prejudge it—just tell me what it is."

"It concerns some experiments that have been carried out by experts in twins. That is, in the science of studying twins..."

Gema's eyes closed once more.

"Very interesting... Go on."

"I'm not joking Gema; to some extent, it is connected to group behavior."

"Alright, I'm listening."

"It has been observed that among persons who are very close, very dependent on one another, it is often the case that in an unconscious manner the partner's state of mind, their reaction to a determined stimulus..."

"That's old: telepathy."

"No, it's not that... at least, not telepathy as it is traditionally understood. It's more like emotional telepathy, if it needs a name."

"Leave its exact name aside, Thondup, and be specific."

"It has been suggested that this takes place at unconscious levels, that this emotional relationship... yes, it might also be called that... exists relatively generally but has not often been studied. It is seen as something natural, something purely emotional, lacking any specific origin. It is described as "a close friendship," "great comradeship," implying a "mutual intuition" that permits each of the persons involved to "guess" what the other is thinking... But one collective—I can't remember the name of its leader—has proposed that this phenomenon has a real basis, that there really is an unconscious inter-communication going on. They tried to carry out an experiment to bring this to a conscious level, in other words..."

"Tell me the result of the experiment, Thondup."

"As you wish... It was carried out with five sets of twins. In three of them, nothing happened. In the other two the experiment provoked violent neurotic reactions."

"Doesn't that prove it's better to abandon this line of thinking, Thondup?"

"That's exactly what they did: they suspended that kind of experiment. But I've been thinking about their basic idea, and it seems to me they made a mistake when they chose the samples for their tests … It was assumed that when the emotional relationship between the subjects was made conscious, it would become even stronger and grow independently of the physical presence of the other twin. In other words, it would be like turning them into mental Siamese twins. So they chose twins, on the basis that their identical genetic make-up would favor a greater closeness in their mental structures, at least deep down. But they overlooked the fact that twins naturally have to struggle to affirm their own identities, their selves, in the face of another almost identical person. They make an effort to differentiate themselves, and so of course resist anything that could fuse them together even more closely…"

"That isn't very clear."

Thondup exploded.

"What do you expect? I'm not a specialist in the study of twins. I found out about all this completely by accident… I'm doing what I can to find a solution here, Gema."

"I know; I'm sorry."

Thondup sank back in his seat and went on:

"In the case of twins, there was no chance of bringing the relationship to a conscious level. But in our case, if Isanusi could only bring our emotional connection to that level, so that in his mind the other members of our group 'came alive,' then I think his mental stability could hold long enough to get back to Earth."

"Now I really don't follow you, Thondup… Alright, let's say that Isanusi can raise that emotional telepathy to a conscious level, but that doesn't take away from the fact that when we two die, all he will have left is the memory, and from what you've been explaining, I don't think that would be enough to…"

Excited, Thondup did not let Gema finish:

"But it would be more than a simple memory. According to Sakharov's theory of mental representation, the impressions we have of our acquaintances are only partial, imprecise, lack their own "life" due to the fact that they are only known to us through their actions, their words, the reflection of their personalities, the consequences of them, rather than the personalities as such. And yet, between people who experience this kind of emotional telepathy, that is not what happens: often, they are capable of "predicting" the future reaction of their "intimate friend" with incredible accuracy, even if it does not coincide with their psychological profile… That was the starting point for the group which carried out the experiment with those sets of twins."

"All this is very interesting as a theoretical debate, but…"

"Wait… I'm just coming to the practical consequences. Emotional telepathy implies a far deeper link than the simple perception of events or physical acts. It is not the reflection of one mind perceived by another but is rather a direct contact. Of course it is not controlled or conscious, but that is what we are trying to correct. It's not a matter of what Isanusi can receive from us now, but examining the possibility of making conscious all his previous intimations of earlier emotional flows that you, me, Pavel, Alix, and Kay have experienced… If we could do that, then the mental representations that Isanusi has of us would lose their partial, imprecise, 'dead' character, and instead become 'autonomous units' that are truly alive, equivalent in practice to what we are ourselves. As you will of course have noted, I am presuming that an emotional telepathy exists within our group. I don't think I need to prove that, because you know the examples as well as I do…" Gema nodded. "I think that those autonomous units must already exist; in a latent, embryonic, incomplete form, of course. But all we have to do is reinforce the emotional telepathy so that it matures, becomes conscious."

Gema considered what she had heard for a relatively short time. Then she asked Thondup,

"All that is fine, but if we give that level of consistency, of reality, to these autonomous units of yours, so that Isanusi continues to see us as alive, wouldn't that distort his perception of reality and make it hard for him to react adequately to any situation that might arise?"

Thondup energetically rejected this.

"No. It is more than a memory but less than a hallucination. Isanusi would be aware that we were no more than phantoms in his mind."

Gema looked inside the pod.

"What do you think of all this, Isanusi?" His lips moved for a longer time, and Gema smiled. She translated for Thondup: "He says that Audo would have liked this solution; it's just crazy and unlikely enough to work…" She straightened up and turned towards Thondup. "He agrees that we should try it; he wants us to get on with the practical part. He especially wants to know what methods the twin experts employed to try to make the emotional telepathy conscious."

"An indirect method, but one that I think is effective. Rather than attempting to make the emotional flows conscious at the moment they occurred, they chose to work with all the accumulated data linked to them stored in the unconscious levels of memory… You don't know this method, but Isanusi does; it's called eidetic induction. I calculate that in his present state, Isanusi could manage to auto-induct himself; he is receiving very few outside stimuli, so they would not interfere.

Besides, I could not induct him; I couldn't do it just through his hearing, and he has no other functioning sensory channels... Gema, ask him if he thinks he can do it."

Gema bent over the pod once more. Then she said out loud:

"He says he will try." She leaned back in her seat, a thoughtful look on her face. "Thondup, couldn't you explain this eidetic induction for me a little? Perhaps I could help somehow..."

The psychosociologist glanced at her doubtfully before replying:

"I don't see how... But I have no problem telling you something about it, Gema. Everyone perceives the world around them as a totality; they systematically accumulate all the information they receive through their senses, even though in practice they are only consciously aware of a small part of this at the moment it is produced—the part their interest is concentrated on. They don't register the rest, but it is stored in their unconscious memory... And the way to reach that is through eidetic induction, which is very similar to a hypnotic trance. The inducted person relives in precise detail episodes from their past, recalling things which, at the moment they took place, escaped their conscious attention... And among those details are included the telepathic emotional perceptions, which, as they were not on a conscious level, went unnoticed by the individual concerned—in this case, Isanusi. Now that he knows they exist, he can search for them, identify them, and consciously order them... That's the result we are hoping for."

Gema cleared her throat, then said,

"Thondup... I don't think we should do this just with Isanusi. After all, I'm sure your twin experts worked simultaneously with both twins."

He hesitated a moment before agreeing.

Gema continued:

"I think our chances of success would be greater if two people tried simultaneously to bring their emotional telepathy to a conscious level. It's very likely it will not be enough to recall past perceptions, but we'll need to put that faculty to the test in practice; that could help speed the process up…"

As Gema spoke, Thondup's brow furrowed. He replied hesitantly:

"Yes… I follow your idea, Gema. But after all that has happened in recent days, I'm not sure I would be able to induct myself."

"So why don't you induct me?"

Thondup's eyes rolled up.

"Gema, you…"

She did not let him finish:

"Yes, I know what you think about my current emotional capacities, and I don't agree, Thondup… And anyway, my memories are in here." She pointed to the side of her head. "For now, at least."

"But…"

"Please, Thondup. Don't tell me it won't work with me." She stood up determinedly from her seat, and said,

"When do we start?"

Part Two

FIRST WITCH: *When shall we three meet again?*
SECOND WITCH: *When the battle's lost and won.*

—William Shakespeare, *Macbeth*

From some obscure but close-by spot came a reassuring, regular sound. She tried to identify it: "A water pump. Yes, a very tired water pump…" She was annoyed: "How can a water pump be tired?" She attuned her other senses, trying to understand… Everything was dark, but it was a pleasant, secure darkness. "How can this be?" She was floating in an invisible liquid, undisturbed by currents and very still. She realized with a shiver that she was not breathing: "Can this be death?" She rejected this absurd thought: "No, death is nothingness…" She tried to bend her arm, to touch herself, confirm her body really existed. She felt its weakness, the lack of coordination in her muscles. They all tried to obey at the same time, contracting spasmodically, jerkily, and creating little whirlpools in the liquid around her. These weak currents slapped against her skin, although she was unsure of exactly where, then slowly died away, until they had completely ceased… She tried desperately to think, to remember: "Where am I? What's happened to me? Who am I?" It was useless to search through her memory; nothing there. She went on floating, outside space and time…

The sudden upheaval hit her from all sides, provoking a wave of irrational panic within her. "What is this?" The water pump was throbbing now with a faster, more violent rhythm that was no longer in any way soothing. The unpleasant sensation gradually eased, leaving her body wracked with pain… and then rushed back, even more intensely. If her throat had obeyed her, if there had been any air in her lungs, she would have shouted out loud. Confusedly, she realized she was rolling over and over in the frothing liquid…

At length she grew accustomed to the sudden onset of the waves of pressure and their slow withdrawal, their increasing frequency, when all at once she felt something hard pressing on her skull. She panicked again, fearing her bones would not withstand it; they were bending, twisting out of shape, while the invisible pressure kept forcing her head against the wall. By now it was an iron ring encircling her temples. She wished above all to lose consciousness, to abandon her tortured body to the inevitable…

She noticed there had been a change; very slowly, the iron ring was moving down to her body and incomprehensibly losing the power it had to squeeze her mercilessly… For the first time, she felt that her wet head was free of pain. A strange sensation was filtering through her still closed eyelids. It took her some time to recognize what it was: "Light…"

Everything faded, and Gema found herself awake, perspiring, recoiling as she gazed at Thondup's worried face. He asked anxiously:

"Are you feeling alright?"

She gestured feebly that she was, and the man's face relaxed.

"I woke you up before I should have. I didn't like the way you looked. What episode were you revisiting?"

Gema moistened her lips before replying.

"I think …" She paused and thought for a moment. "No, I'm sure of it; I was being born again."

Thondup clicked his tongue with disappointment.

"That's too far back …" He helped Gema sit up.

"Don't worry, it often happens in the first inductions. You have to explore before you can properly locate the period of time you're aiming for."

Massaging the nape of her neck with both hands, Gema asked,

"Let's try again, Thondup."

The psychosociologist shook his head. He pointed to the nearest control panel.

"Don't forget him; I don't know much about medicine, but I don't like the figures I can see there."

Gema stood up quickly and looked at them. She pursed her lips.

"You're right. Are the instruments prepared?"

He nodded.

"Let's go then."

Her right hand moved rapidly, aiming the tip of the slender cylinder first in one direction, then another. The flesh separated gently, revealing bones and tendons. The other hand, equipped with a curved blade, was prizing apart skin, muscle, and cartilage that had already been sliced through, leaving the carotids and the jugular exposed … Gema laid the laser-scalpel on the table beside her. She took a pair of pincers and gripped the bottom part of the jugular, pulling it slightly out of the surrounding tissue. Her left hand had let go of the blade and was now holding a thin transparent tube, on the tip of which gleamed a hollow needle. She pushed the needle upwards into the thick vein, at the same time finishing the incision on the torn jugular with her other hand. She squirted the lisosol between the tube and the vein. Inside the transparent pipe the blood was visible as it rose in short, rapid bursts towards the receptacle on top of the reanimator… From that point on, Thondup was unable to follow the agile movements of Gema's hands around the carotids; he was too busy concentrating on carefully wiping off all the sweat that had collected on his companion's eyebrows and was threatening to drip into her eyes. When he next looked at what had once been Isanusi's neck, another two tubes had been firmly attached to the carotids. A reddish liquid remotely similar to blood was flowing through them. Breathing heavily, Gema stepped back from the pod.

"Tired?" Thondup asked.

She shook her head. She added,

"No… Now we just have to wait to see if his brain will accept the artificial blood."

Thondup nodded silently. They both sat down. A few minutes later, Gema continued:

"In any case, I need to recover my strength… What comes next takes speed and great precision. I can't make any mistakes…"

Thondup interrupted her:

"His heart has stopped, Gema."

Gema leapt up beside the pod. She examined the transparent pipes… and smiled.

"You were wrong, Thondup: it's working fine."

"I don't mean the new one…"

"Oh, the old one…" She glanced inside the pod and shrugged.

The laser-scalpel moved rapidly, almost casually, along the median line of the skull from the nape to between the eyes. Following it at a similar speed came the ultrasonic knife, leaving behind it a clean cut through the bone. Thondup could not help calling out,

"Be careful, Gema."

Pausing the operation, she looked at him in surprise:

"Careful about what…?" Beneath the mask covering the lower half of her face, a slight smile was visible.

"Alright, I understand. The ultrasound's frequency is determined by the thickness of the bone. There's no danger to the brain."

The laser-scalpel cut through the skin again, closely followed as before by the ultrasonic knife. They reached the top part of the ear, then descended along the hairline to the nape of the neck. The two knives turned again and reached the starting point once more. Gema laid the blades aside and carefully lifted the cut section of the skull. Man and woman gazed down at the pale pink membrane covering the brain. Gema commented:

"Now comes the hard part. Pay attention, Thondup."

Picking up the laser scalpel once more, she carefully aimed for each of the areas where spreading stains indicated that the capillaries had been damaged… The stains stopped spreading. Then the ultrasonic knife came into play again, getting rid of the bone surrounding the medulla and the nerves. The laser-scalpel immediately cut off any new mini-hemorrhages.

"Quickly: the micro-operator and the terminals."

Thondup handed her what she was calling for. Gema adjusted the micro-operator around the medulla. She warned Thondup,

"Be ready to dry the area."

She manipulated the controls, and the mini-laser circled the medulla, cutting the exterior membrane. The upper edge was still stuck to the lower ones, as microscopic clamps grasped the lower part and drew it downwards, exposing the bundle of nerves and releasing the cerebrospinal fluid… Thondup slipped a piece of absorbent foam under the medulla, and the slow threads of dark liquid disappeared.

"The first terminal, please."

The laser of the micro-operator had advanced into the medulla, and already cut through a bundle of nerves. Thondup pushed in the fine cable she had asked for, and tiny needles sewed the tip to the severed nerves. A miniscule cloud of lisosol appeared and disappeared over the first link between brain and bio-computer, as the laser advanced another millimeter.

Gema's fingers were scarcely caressing the controls. A moment later, and another small cloud of lisosol puffed out.

"The third…"

Wearily, Thondup leaned on the edge of the pod. Gema immediately froze. Raising her eyes from the viewfinder, she stared hard at him and warned,

"Sit down if you're tired, but don't touch the pod." Her eyes returned to the viewfinder, and she requested,

"The fourteenth one, please…"

Thondup pushed in the required terminal and sat down, breathing heavily. He asked, "Is there much longer to go?"

Gema replied, without looking at him,

"One hour. Maybe two. No more questions. Just give me the fifteenth."

Thondup meekly inserted the terminal and said nothing more.

"This is the last one, Gema," said Thondup, with obvious satisfaction. Gema did not respond.

The micro-needles finished joining the terminal to the left optic nerve. Gema stiffened, revealing her swollen eyes; the viewfinder had left two circular purple welts. She staggered across to the nearest chair and collapsed into it. Closing her eyes, she smiled weakly:

"I only hope I didn't get any of the connections wrong… or anything else." She felt for the arm of the chair, and it immediately tilted backwards. She went on talking, now lying flat. "You'll have to finish the job yourself; I don't think I can move for another two hours... Put a pair of gloves on..."

The man's fingers awkwardly pushed into the white material.

"Ready, Gema."

"Take the brain in your hands... Carefully now, don't drop it, whatever you do. Carry it to the container..." She listened carefully to Thondup's footsteps across the polyfoam. She instructed him again: "Put it in upside down, with the terminals facing upwards, otherwise it won't fit... Done that?"

"Yes, that's done."

"Can you see two blue conductors next to the container?"

"Yes, I can..."

"Get hold of them and push the needles on the ends into the dura mater. Don't worry, they won't reach the brain, it's all been calculated ... Try to place them as far apart as possible."

Holding a tube in each hand, Thondup hesitated. He asked, "What's this for?"

Gema opened her eyes and stared at him, irritated.

"Stop asking so many questions and do it."

Thondup agreed reluctantly, and Gema's gaze softened slightly.

"Silly idiot... We need to replace the cerebrospinal fluid between the membranes and the brain; that's what the tubes are for. We have to do things properly or not do them at all... Cover the container. You'll see there's a semicircular hole on the outside; lay the terminals and tubes there."

She watched him doing all this. She said approvingly,

"Very good. Now open the regulator switch on the green tank."

This time Thondup did not ask her anything but did as she said. A yellowish liquid slowly filled the container. The brain wobbled, turned, was covered… then floated, swaying slightly, in the liquid.

"Now seal the hole with lisosol… Yes, I know it's not ideal, but there's nothing else. Or am I mistaken?"

"No, you're not mistaken. Anything more?"

"Yes, keep an eye on the dials for a few minutes to make sure all the readings are normal… Then take the body away."

"To the refuse chute?"

"That would be best. It's going to decompose very quickly."

"Alright, now get some rest…"

"Wait, then come back and keep watching the brain…"

"Yes, I know, until you're restored."

"Correct."

Thondup saw her face suddenly relax. He looked at her closely; her skin looked even more pallid, making the petechiae dotted all over it even more conspicuous. He let out a sigh. "It's a normal reaction. Too much tension. Even if she had been healthy, she wouldn't have been able to continue." His gaze transferred to the monitor. "Everything fine up to now; as long as Isanusi doesn't discover that … No, there's no reason he should realize. The best guarantee is the willingness to believe it…" Settling back in the seat, he concentrated on the dials.

Raising her head, Gema looked around in a dazed fashion. When she saw Thondup, her eyes lit up.

"Did I sleep for long?"

Thondup looked over his shoulder at her, then returned to the screen. He replied,

"Not enough. Barely four hours."

"That's a lot, Thondup."

He swiveled his chair around until he was facing her, and asked,

"How long was it since you last slept, Gema?"

"I don't remember... Not since the 'grey' incident, I think."

Thondup nodded thoughtfully.

"Yes... I don't think this was a normal sleep, I'd almost call it losing consciousness when your mind became overloaded..."

Gema tried to stand up and eventually succeeded. Smiling, she walked a few steps. She said with no great emotion,

"That's probable... Have you eaten?"

"I was waiting for you."

"Very kind of you. Shall we?"

In response, Thondup offered her his arm. Gema clung to him, leaning most of her weight on him. She apologized:

"I still feel a bit weak..."

"It doesn't matter; I can bear it."

They walked towards the restroom.

"Thondup, did you take the psychostabilizer?"

"At the required time, don't worry."

A mocking gleam appeared in her eyes.

"It wouldn't be a bad thing if you forgot occasionally... There's lots of the ship that still needs painting."

Thondup looked despondent:

"That's not going to happen, Gema, There are no sprays left."

They were still laughing as they entered the room.

Thondup came out of the bathroom, drying his face. He grunted:

"I'm passing liquid again, Gema."

"I was expecting as much; I calculate it'll be my turn tomorrow..."

She moved to one side, leaving him space in the bed. Thondup lay down wearily and closed his eyes...

"Thondup..."

"What is it?"

"Couldn't you induct me now?"

His eyebrows were raised a little, then fell again. He drew a hand across his face and opened his eyes. He said,

"Gema, you've had enough for one day."

"Just for a minute… I have to practice whenever I can; we don't have much time, as you well know."

Muttering to himself, Thondup sat up in the bed.

…Pulling harder, she finally got Isanusi out of the hypnotron. He fell on top of her… She was panting, exhausted, beneath the inert body. "There's nothing else for it; I'll have to use my reserves." Which she did.

The energy flowed to her muscles. She was able to stand up and haul the unconscious man along by the arms. Stumbling, falling, getting up again, she made her way down the corridor to the sick bay. "How heavy you are, my love." She paused to get her breath back. Sitting on the floor, she settled the curly head on her lap and caressed it… "You're breathing normally; it can't be anything serious. I only have to get you to the diagnostic machine and…" She got to her feet and began dragging the heavy body along again…

"Well?"

"Too close this time, Thondup."

"When exactly?"

"After the collision with the meteorite."

He gave a brief nod.

"Fine. Now we have two reference points. Next time..."

"Please, Thondup. I feel very tired. Let's continue tomorrow."

She stretched out on the bed, closing her eyes and relaxing her body... Thondup hesitated before saying,

"Gema..."

"What?"

"While you were in your eidetic state, I think there was another meteorite; the ship changed course again."

"Oh no, not now."

"I don't think it's urgent. Rest now, you can correct it tomorrow..."

Moving slowly and heavily, Gema sat up in bed.

"Thanks, Thondup, but it has to be now."

She strode unsteadily towards the door and leaned against it.

"Before I forget... Thondup, reduce the gravity field to 0.8G."

Thondup tried to get up quickly but almost fell to the floor. Gema told him,

"It doesn't have to be right now; you can leave it until tomorrow, it's not a change of direction."

He waited for his dizziness to recede before replying:

"No, it has to be now... Otherwise you might not get back to bed."

He stood up but had to support himself against the wall.

"I don't know what's happening to me... My head starts reeling whenever I try to do something..."

Gema's eyebrows closed in a frown.

"You move too quickly, that's all," she said. "Think before you begin any movement. Any unexpected gesture is bound to make you feel dizzy... Let's see if you've understood. Walk over here."

Thondup walked slowly, haltingly. Gema nodded.

"That's right."

She moved away from the hatch and down the corridor.

With bated breath, a smile glinting in her eyes, Gema pushed the door open a couple of inches. A shaft of light beamed onto half her face. She blinked as her eyes grew accustomed to the brightness. She saw a woman sitting beside a table covered in flowers, talking to someone she could not see:

"...I won't tell her."

"Then I will."

Gema recognized the voice: "Papa, I mustn't..." She pulled the door slowly towards her, closing it. Her mother went on:

"Neither you nor me; Gema isn't to know."

Standing by the narrow crack still showing in the doorway, the person they were talking about caught her breath.

"The letter is addressed to her, Luz; it's completely illegal to keep it from her—she's an adult now..."

"An adult? Because she has just turned fourteen? She's still a child, and she has no idea what's best for her."

"But you do, naturally."

The voices fell silent. Without meaning to, Gema pushed the door open a little further. She could see her father standing by the window, staring out into the night...

Raising her damp eyes to him, her mother said,

"You've got no feelings. Don't you know how dangerous it is?"

"There's always danger everywhere, Luz."

"Not compared to this. If you know so much, why don't you tell me what happened to the last expedition?"

Her father's fingers had been drumming on the windowsill. Now the noise stopped. He turned to her, frowning.

"Nobody knows."

"Aha... Just imagine for a moment that Gema had been there, on that expedition." Her mother stretched out a trembling hand to the flowers on the table. She picked out a rose, still gazing at the father. She began plucking the petals, one by one. "Perhaps they're still alive and can't find a way to return... Would you be able to bear it if you were the father of one of them?"

"That's happening now. By the time Gema has grown up, spaceships will be safer. And we will know more about the Solar System. Events like this will be impossible."

"Like this, I'm sure they will be, but there will be far worse. Can't you see they will always be travelling further, penetrating the unknown and coming across new and greater dangers? Or don't you have the foresight to see that either?"

When he replied, the father's tone was uncertain.

"In any case, many—the vast majority—do return... Besides, it's very unlikely she will become part of a cosmogroup. Apparently only one in ten who enter the Academy finishes the training."

Her mother shook her head vigorously.

"No, that argument doesn't convince me, my love. They haven't selected anyone from that precosmic group for the Academy for twelve years—twelve years!—and now they choose Gema. I don't want to tempt fate again. Once is enough."

The father crossed the room and sat beside the mother. He looked at her, bewildered.

"I don't understand you, Luz. You were the one who insisted that Gema join the precosmic group. That was when you should have considered all this..."

"You don't want to understand. Nobody was ever selected from that group, and where else could Gema receive such good training?"

The woman's voice had taken on a hysterical tone. Stretching across the flowers, the man tapped her affectionately on the back.

"Alright, alright... Please don't cry. We won't say anything to her.

But what if they come here to find out why she hasn't turned up at the Academy?"

His wife's eyes glinted.

"There's no reason for them to come. They'll assume she doesn't want to go... I'll reply to their notification myself, explaining that Gema doesn't want to go to the Academy."

The man raised his eyebrows doubtfully.

"What if they want to talk to her?"

"Why shouldn't they trust me? Aren't I her mother?"

"Luz..."

"I won't listen to any more. She's not going to find out."

"Don't fool yourself. She'll get to know sooner or later."

"Alright, she'll get to know... but too late."

"She won't forgive you."

"Oh, I know what she's like; she won't speak to me for a couple of days, perhaps a week, but everything will return to normal."

The father closed his eyes and leaned back in his chair.

"I'm not sure... It's her life, her great opportunity, Luz."

"She'll have other less dangerous ones. That's enough arguing, Gema must be about to come back. Give me the notification."

Something white and shiny changed hands... Gema closed the door silently. She walked towards the stairs, deep in thought. By the time she started to climb, her mind was made up. She went to her room, peered for a moment at the starry sky outside the window, then began to take her clothes from the wardrobe with rapid, decisive movements.

Thondup's face became clearer, his features more precise... A thought passed through her mind almost instinctively: "How thin he's become." Anticipating his questions, Gema told him,

"Quite close this time, Thondup. The day before I joined the Academy… You know the episode—when my parents tried to stop me going."

Thondup nodded.

"We can't be more accurate, Gema. From there you'll have to go forward in a straight line."

"Thondup, one thing worries me: I did not get any sense of emotional flows between my parents and me… But they must have existed, at least at that moment. They were really upset by the situation, and so was I."

The psychosociologist shook his head.

"No. In a case like that, you could not expect to sense their emotional flows, Gema; their wishes and yours did not coincide… Besides, I have to warn you that you won't find it so easy to perceive other people's emotions." Standing up, he repeated: "No, it's not easy…"

Behind the spectacles, a slightly puzzled look appeared on the woman's smiling face. She glanced through the files, still talking:

"Gema… Yes, Gema; here it is." Picking up a piece of paper, she studied it closely, and her smile broadened. "I see… In fact, we were expecting you tomorrow." She looked up inquisitively at the girl sitting opposite her desk. "There must have been some mistake with your notification."

Gema felt a dryness in her throat… Her expression must have betrayed some of her emotion, because the woman quickly added,

"It doesn't matter. Could I see it now?"

Gema swallowed hard before replying:

"I haven't got it with me; I left it at home."

The woman looked even more puzzled. Her eyes moved between Gema and her ID card… She shrugged slightly.

"Well, that's not important." She smiled again. "I'll see if I can find your instructor." She glanced quickly again at the sheet of paper in her hand. "Audo… wait a minute." She bent over the intercom and said, "Valia, find out where Audo is and tell him I need him…" Muffled sounds that Gema could not follow came over the intercom. The woman at the desk made a sour face and spoke again to the invisible Valia: "When he appears, tell him one of his group is already here." The intercom gave out more garbled noises, and the woman replied, "Don't worry, I'll take her to her room. Thanks." Switching the intercom off, she got up from her seat. She said to Gema, "Come with me."

Gema stood up with her suitcase. Seeing this for the first time, the woman said with surprise,

"But… you brought clothes with you?"

Gema nodded silently. The woman shook her head and grumbled:

"Your notification must have been incomplete: it should have clearly stated you would not need them…" She looked at the newcomer's face and obviously realized how nervous she was, because she quickly added, "Oh well, it's not serious. We can send the case back… Of course, if there's anything special in it, some memento you'd like to keep…" Gema signaled that there was nothing like that in it. "Alright, leave it here then."

Gema put the case down next to the desk and followed the woman down the wide corridor.

"Look…" Without slowing up, her newfound guide pointed outside the large windows that filled the left-hand wall: "That's the park; a good place to have a rest… Beyond it are the trainees' sleeping quarters. That's where yours is too." Gema craned her neck to try to see the buildings, but the woman told her, "You can't see them, they're hidden by the trees… Ah, and before I forget, you are in 23-J. Remember that, it's the number of your group as well."

"23-J; 23-J; 23-J…"

Half a dozen girls and boys came down the corridor, chatting and laughing. When they saw the pair approaching them, they fell silent, examining Gema with a mixture of curiosity and sympathy. One of the boys called out,

"Is this a new girl? Look after her, Stella, don't scare her…"

Gema felt her cheeks flushing. Stella wagged her finger at the boy, but could not help smiling:

"You're the one who would scare her, Alex. Keep going, and hurry up, Irina's been looking for you for an hour."

The youngsters glanced at each other, then almost broke into a run. Still smiling, Stella watched them go and told Gema:

"They are group 11-H… Watch your step with them, they like to fool around too much." She touched the wall, and it opened in front of them. She gestured for Gema to step inside. "Go on in."

The elevator door slid shut behind them, and immediately they began a gentle descent… From out of nowhere, a toneless voice announced,

"It has started to rain."

Stella's brow wrinkled.

"That's a shame… I'd have liked to show you the woods; they're really nice. I love going for a stroll there… Well, you'll have time enough to explore."

The elevator door opened, and they walked out into the hall of the Central Building. They crossed it, with Stella exchanging greetings to right and left, until they came to another door. She explained to Gema, "It's best if we go by the subway."

There were no windows in this next corridor. Stella came to a halt beside one of the green belts that stretched all along it, and motioned for Gema to stand beside her. She said out loud,

"J... 23."

The floor began to move, at increasing speed... Instinctively, Gema clung to Stella's arm. The older woman glanced over her shoulder at her and smiled.

"You'll soon get used to it, my dear."

The conveyor belt gradually slowed down and came to a stop. Stella went across to the nearest door and opened it, revealing another smaller elevator.

"In you go."

They came out into a medium-sized room. Opposite the elevator was a glass wall. Through it Gema could see pine trees whipped by the squally rain. She gave a sharp intake of breath.

"Beautiful, isn't it? And you're not in D block; the rooms there are by the lake. That really is a spectacular view..." Stella had crossed the room as she talked. She slid back a multi-colored partition, and another room appeared.

"This is the girls' dormitory, for now." She pressed a button by the door, and a rectangle appeared in the wall.

"This is your wardrobe; you can change your clothes anytime."

Gema walked over to the brilliantly-colored tunics and felt them softly... Stella was sitting on the nearest bed, smiling at her.

"If you have any questions to ask, feel free."

The cloth slipped through Gema's fingers.

"Do you know Audo?" she asked. A gleam of comprehension appeared in Stella's eyes. She shook her head:

"No, he's new too. You're the first group he is going to train. But you needn't worry, I've never known any group that didn't idolize their instructor…" She broke off and covered her left ear with her hand. She listened intently for a moment. She nodded in agreement as if the person she was speaking to could see her, then said to Gema: "You're in luck, you're not the only member of your group to arrive early. I've just been told another girl is here." She stood up from the bed. "I have to go and greet her." She walked rapidly over to the elevator door but stopped halfway there and looked back quizzically at Gema. "Would you like to come with me…? Or do you prefer to wait for her here?"

It took Gema some time to respond.

"I'll wait for her here."

Stella nodded understandingly and entered the elevator. The door closed. Gema was alone in the large room. She walked slowly over to the wall of glass and stared for a long while at the raindrops sliding down the smooth surface, blurring the view of the pines… She turned when she heard Stella's voice again:

"…and this is Gema."

Out of the elevator stepped a small, blonde girl with a round, smiling face. Stella excused herself:

"Forgive me, but I can't stay any longer, I have lots of work to do…"

The elevator door slid shut. The blonde girl and Gema stared at each other, slightly embarrassed… The new arrival stepped forward, held out her hand and introduced herself simply:

"I'm Alix."

A luminous dot was moving up and down the screen at irregular intervals… Gema commented:

"As you can see, it's impossible to draw any conclusions from that."

Thondup nodded.

"But we can at least see that his brain is functioning, Gema."

He pointed to the dot with his finger.

"Strong, rhythmic waves... He must be conscious."

"Do you think he managed to induct himself?"

Thondup looked doubtful.

"It's possible... As I recall, he knew the technique well."

Chewing her bottom lip, Gema asked,

"Do you think I can do it on my own by now?"

Thondup gazed at her thoughtfully.

"You could try..."

The man stood up from his chair, pressing his hands on the desk. He was small and looked rather portly. He had slanting eyes and straight hair already receding in front. "I don't like him," thought Gema. Suddenly feeling awkward, she shifted in her seat. At that moment, Audo began to speak:

"Very good... Now we all know each other... by sight at least. We have several years ahead of us to establish a more solid relationship and a common goal: to make sure you are a group."

He paced up and down the room, hands clasped behind his back, peering intently into their eyes... Gema looked away.

"To be a group, or more correctly, to become a group... Really, as yet we know very little about how this process happens. It's true that your psychological profiles indicate that you are capable of doing so. But the same is true of all the proto-groups that arrive at the Academy, and only a few, a very few, achieve it. Naturally, I would like you to succeed." He came to a halt in front of them, legs slightly apart. "To be frank, I must tell you I don't have much experience. Or rather, none at all. But they..."—he gestured with his shoulder towards the nearest wall—have consulted the computers and tell me that I can be successful with you. It's not a certainty, of course, only a slightly greater possibility than with the other instructors. Now it all depends on you, and if you truly want to be a cosmogroup... Do you want that?"

A ragged murmur of agreement could be heard, while Gema merely nodded her head... Audo let out a sigh.

"I hope that what you feel inside is more intense than what you've expressed out loud... Anyway, let's move on to the crux of the problem, as I see it: What does being a group, a real group, actually mean?" He looked around the room; nobody said a word. "It means that its members agree on all the fundamentals and disagree on everything else." He stressed the word "everything." "In fact, this definition merely shifts the problem rather than resolving it: what is meant by the "fundamentals," and what is "everything else"? In my view, each group has to find its own answer to that question. Its own answer: each of the cosmogroups I have been involved with has its own character, its specific way of looking at and doing things... We would not resolve anything if we imitated what others have done; we need to discover what we have to do in our case."

He paused. He saw their thoughtful faces and concluded:

"That's enough for today; I don't want to overwhelm you on your first day here. I'll be happy if you start to think about this problem..."

He had gradually moved over to the elevator. He opened the door.

"Should you need to see me for any reason, all you have to do is press this button," he pointed to it, "and I'll come as quickly as possible." He stepped into the elevator. The small, thickset boy with mongoloid features ("What's his name...?" Gema remembered the future: "Ah, Thondup.") stepped forward, raising an arm. Audo halted, his hand on the elevator controls.

Stammering slightly, Thondup asked,

"And what... what are we supposed to do now?"

A broad smile appeared on Audo's face. Gema thought, "He's not so terrible after all." The instructor answered Thondup: "Get to know each other; go for a walk in the woods, talk to one another… By tomorrow you'll be protesting that you don't have a minute free."

With that, the elevator door closed.

Thondup's eyes reflected his curiosity and surprise. He murmured,

"Well, it's true that subjective time passes more quickly than real time in eidetic states… but not so quickly, Gema."

She sat down in the seat.

"That's not important, Thondup. What I want is to go as fast as possible. We don't have much time, and you know it."

"Yes, I know…" He fell silent for a moment, then declared,

"To be frank, I didn't like Audo much that first day."

Gema agreed:

"Nor did I."

Alix's eyes glinted in the darkness. Gema asked,

"What do you want?"

Alix slipped into Gema's bed like a frightened ghost before replying,

"I feel very alone…"

A lump rose in Gema's throat. All she could think was: "So do I." Wrapping her arm around Alix's back, she snuggled up to her… All at once, another shadow came between the bed and the dim nighttime glow coming through the window. Gema felt Alix's back muscles tauten. In a whisper, she asked,

"Who's there?"

"Who do you think?"

Gema recognized Kay's irritated voice.

"You two get together, and everything's fine, just perfect. Let Kay look after herself, on her own…" She clambered into the bed, still protesting: "The least you could do is leave me a bit of room, isn't it?"

Gema squashed up against the wall, and Alix moved over a little towards the center and turned on her side. That was the only way there was room for Kay on the edge of the bed… It wasn't long before they heard Alix's muffled voice:

"You're going to suffocate me… Why don't we bring over another bed? One's not enough for the three of us."

Gema agreed immediately.

"Alix is right, Kay; let's get out."

In the darkness, three half-dressed figures clustered around the middle bed. They tried moving it but failed. Panting, Kay sat on the edge and muttered,

"It's no good; we can't shift it… We'll have to get the boys' help."

Alix replied, unconvinced:

"It's very late, Kay; they must be asleep by now."

There was enough light for the other two to make out Kay's smile.

"Are you sure?"

"Of course; they're not as well-behaved as us. Right, Gema?"

Gema looked uncertainly towards the door.

"Well, I'm not sure… We'd have to see."

"Let's go and see then," said Kay, striding out of the room. Still doubtful, Gema and Alix followed her. They caught up with her just as she was knocking on the door to the boys' room. A wide-awake voice called out from the far side:

"Who is it?"

"It's the girls, can we come in?" Ignoring Alix's and Gema's waving arms, she went on: "Are you decent?" and opened the door.

The three boys were sitting on the windowsill, their legs dangling out. Taken by surprise, they peered over their shoulders at the youngsters invading their dormitory. Before they could get over their shock, Kay asked,

"We need help to push two beds together; can you do it?"

"We could certainly do it... but why do you need to push them together?" Pavel jumped down and came over to the girls, gazing at them curiously. Kay sternly held his look.

"If you have to be so inquisitive..."

Gema protested:

"You're being unfair, Kay. If we're asking for their help, it's only natural we tell them why." She turned towards the three boys coming over to them, adjusting the scant clothing they had on and explained: "The thing is, we feel lonely; we want to sleep together, but one bed isn't big enough for the three of us."

Isanusi burst out laughing. Thondup frowned and scolded him:

"I don't see why you're laughing. They're girls, so it's logical that..."

"Laughing at them? No, Thondup, at all of us..."

Isanusi addressed the girls: "We also miss our precosmic groups, so we know what you mean. Of course we can help you."

Joking and laughing, the six headed for the girls' dormitory. The boys moved to one side of the bed and pushed together as hard as they could... but it did not move. In an apparently innocent voice, Kay said,

"I think we're going to have to call Audo..."

Wiping the sweat from his brow, Pavel suggested,

"Perhaps it's nailed to the floor?"

Isanusi shook his head.

"I don't think so. I got the impression it moved slightly." He looked thoughtfully at the faces around him. "But I'm thinking that what is too heavy for three girls or three boys might not be too much for six. Shall we give it a try?"

"Let's try," said Gema and went to stand next to him. Kay and Alix did likewise, and the six of them pushed in unison. Creaking and groaning, the bed moved in short jerks until it was up against Gema's. As soon as she had got her breath back, Kay offered:

"If you'd like us to help you push two beds together, boys..."

Out of the corner of his eye, Thondup replied curtly,

"Thank you all the same, but there's no need."

Recalling all this had brought a smile to Thondup's face.

"I think that was the first time the six of us worked together with a common aim. Do you think it was a coincidence those beds were so heavy, Gema?"

Seated on the fallen pine needles, his back against the trunk, Audo was staring at the red horizon. Gema came up to him slowly and hesitantly... The instructor's head turned towards her, and he smiled.

"Welcome, Gema." He straightened up and made room for her. "If you'd like to sit down..."

"Yes, I would. Thanks."

She sat next to him, and the they watched the sun set in silence.

Standing in front of the monitor, Gema scrutinized the dials... Thondup inquired:

"Is everything alright?"

"Yes, I think we could try now."

She switched something off, then spoke slowly and clearly:

"Isanusi, this is Gema. Don't try to reply yet…" She looked inquiringly across at Thondup. The psychosociologist nodded.

"We're testing the functioning of your auditory receptors. Listen carefully; if you can hear us, clench your right fist."

A red light came on in the center of the screen.

"Very good… Now open it."

The light went out. The corners of Gema's mouth relaxed slightly.

Sketching a conciliatory smile, the man said,

"Well… Perhaps you're right." Glancing at the watch on his ring, his expression changed to one of surprise: "Goodness… I didn't think it had gotten so late." With an apologetic shrug, he concluded: "I have to go now; it's a shame I can't go on talking to you… Goodbye."

He walked off quickly down the path. When he turned a bend and disappeared from view, the youngsters stared at each other in bewilderment and finally all turned towards Audo. He had a vacant look on his face, as if he were daydreaming. Thondup said,

"An unusual sort, isn't he?"

Audo came out of his dream and looked at him.

"No, Thondup. Unfortunately he's not so unusual."

Kay was watching him, intrigued.

"Do you know him from before, Audo?"

Sitting on a stump, the instructor laid the rucksack across his knees.

"Not him exactly, Kay. But I know the kind he belongs to only too well, unfortunately…"

"There's a story behind this," guessed Gema. Glancing up at the sky to judge the height of the sun, she proposed,

"We could camp here, it's already late."

Audo agreed absent-mindedly.

"Yes, it's not a bad spot..." He went on, as if to himself: "No doubt about it, he's an authentic Neanderthal."

"A what?" inquired Alix.

"A Neanderthal: ne-an-der-thal."

"Neanderthal?" Thondup repeated, taken aback. "I thought they were extinct... Are you sure you aren't mistaken, Audo? To judge by his appearance, he's a Homo sapiens."

"Don't judge by appearances; they can be deceptive," Audo warned him. "It's true that the Neanderthals became extinct a long time ago, but there are still lots who have not changed at all inside since then..."

Isanusi slipped off his rucksack, put it on the ground, and sat on it. He asked,

"Audo, I think you'd better explain what you mean."

The instructor undid his bag and started to take packages out of it. While he was placing them in orderly piles, he said,

"I mean that there are still people whose interests are limited to those of the extinct Neanderthals: that is, to eat, drink, couple with the opposite sex, and to possess shiny, flashy objects..."

"Yes, I know that type: the ones who are all too concerned with the outside world and almost completely ignore their interior life," said Isanusi.

Pavel scratched his head.

"You may be right... But I don't think there are lots of them; at least, he's the first one I've ever seen in my life."

Isanusi smiled.

"I'm not surprised in your case, Pavel. You were born and brought up in one of the oldest lands in the Federation, the environment least likely to encourage the modern Neanderthals... But remember, neither Audo nor me had such luck."

Audo nodded thoughtfully.

"What you say is true, Isanusi... But you need to take into account that examples as obvious as the one we just met are rare these days. You shouldn't underestimate the Neanderthals' capacity to adapt. They know how to take on the most convenient external appearance to allow them to go on enjoying their small appetites and ambitions... That can help you identify them: in general they look unexceptional, but they are afraid, very afraid of losing what they have accumulated, what they possess... For them, there is nothing worse than the possibility of losing their material or social possessions. All those who fight for an ideal are their sworn enemies, and they have given them a name that they see as an insult: "the awkward ones," because they don't compromise when they should, don't stay silent when it would be better for them to do so... They can't understand that at all. To them, the only worthwhile ideal is oneself. Yes, the Neanderthals are really dangerous; they know how to defend themselves. They have kept the their primate ancestors' ability to climb. They can and do cause harm..."

Thondup was pitching the tent. With his back to the group, he commented,

"I bet that all of you were called "awkward." "He turned to face Audo, the guy ropes wrapped around his left wrist. "Or am I mistaken, Audo?"

"No, you're not mistaken."

"Tell us the story, please."

"It's a long and complicated one, Kay..." He looked her in the face, then gave way. "Alright... I can start at the time I became an instructor..." He took out his pipe and filled it with tobacco. As a precaution, Kay moved to one side, out of the way of any possible smoke trail.

"First of all, you have to remember what Isanusi said: the land where I was born has only recently entered the Federation. Some people thought instructors were there to mold docile sheep, to create new Neanderthals..."

A humorous gleam appeared in Kay's eyes.

"I'm afraid they must have been disappointed in you, Audo."

By now, the instructor had lit his pipe. He nodded, puffing smoke.

"I think so too, Kay." He smiled. "That was how I learned they really are dangerous... I had many bad moments. So many in fact that when I was called for the final meeting, I thought I had failed. I said to myself, "They've won, Audo; get used to it." But at that meeting I was told I had been selected as an instructor at the Academy."

Pavel smiled and said,

"I guess the Neanderthals were infuriated by that."

Audo shook his head.

"Oh, no. They had achieved their goal; I would no longer be able to create "awkward ones" among their own flocks." He blew out another mouthful of smoke and watched as it rose into the sky and dispersed. "I have to thank them though for this smoking habit of mine—it calms the nerves..." He glanced at Pavel.

"That was why I found it so hard to accept the job at the Academy."

Pavel stared at him open-mouthed. He managed to say,

"Why?"

"I had a lot of accounts to settle with them... And the best way of doing that was to stay where I was, creating "awkward" people."

"So what made you decide to enter the Academy?"

Audo's face betrayed no emotion as he looked across at Gema.

"In fact, I'm still not sure... Perhaps the decisive factor was fear."

"Fear?"

"Yes, fear. I already told you that the Neanderthals are very dangerous… Up to then, I had been protected for several reasons; above all, by the fact that they never take a risk unless it's absolutely essential for their own safety, Pavel. If I had stayed there and refused to go to the Academy, they would have seen it as open provocation."

Isanusi broke the silence that had followed Audo's last words:

"Audo, I don't understand: why are you always trying to appear worse than you really are?"

The instructor shrugged.

"If that's how you want to see it…"

Standing up, he went over to Thondup and took the tent ropes from him. "Come on, I'll help you with the tent." Raising his eyes, he observed the dark clouds gathering on the horizon. "I have no desire to get soaked tonight."

Gema shook her head of thick hair despondently.

"It's not working, Thondup. Let's try with number twenty-five."

Sighing, the cybernetics expert changed two cables and said,

"Ready, Gema."

She spoke into the monitor:

"Listen, Isanusi: we're going to try again. Is that alright with you?"

The red light came on in agreement.

"Good… Now bend your left leg again. Did you hear that? The left one. Without contracting the calf muscles, please."

Several seconds went by… Nothing appeared on the screen.

"Did you try it?"

The red light flashed on and off; Gema turned to Thondup.

"It's not that one either; we'll have to try again."

Thondup's jaw clenched, and he said nothing.

"Just once more, Thondup. It has to be terminal number twenty-four... I can't have got things so wrong."

His hands darted in among the mass of cables and changed the position of two of them.

"Ready..."

"Isanusi, are you set?"

The red light blinked again.

"Bend your left leg..."

A yellowish light came on at the bottom of the screen, and the worry lines disappeared from Gema's brow.

"Fine... You can straighten your leg again, Isanusi."

The golden glow faded.

The elevator doors closed behind Audo. Pavel was the first to speak.

"To think that a whole year has passed... and it still seems as if it was only yesterday we met..."

Kay squeezed his hand affectionately before disagreeing:

"No, Pavel, that's not right... Only a year, but to me it feels as if we have been together all our lives."

Alix said thoughtfully, "I don't know whether the psychosociologists will agree with me, but I think we're becoming a group, as Audo says."

Isanusi said,

"Audo..." There was something in his voice that made all the others turn towards him. "I wouldn't trade instructors with anyone."

Thondup agreed, choosing his words carefully: "He is very good. He's never lied to us... about what's really important, I mean."

Still staring at the pine trees on the far side of the window, Pavel added,

"I don't think we would have become what we are without him ..."

"What do you think, Gema?"

With a shiver, Gema glanced at Kay.

"Me? ... Yes, he is good."

Her response led to an awkward silence, finally broken by Alix:

"All of you—we ought to find some way to celebrate this anniversary..."

Thondup was gazing up at some point on the ceiling.

"Yes, I remember the group's first anniversary well... Did Alix already know about your feelings for Isanusi?"

"Yes."

"And Audo?"

"Audo? No, not yet."

Thondup smiled.

"The one who's closest is always the last to know."

Getting up from the bed, he walked slowly over to the bathroom.

Without looking at him, Gema replied,

"What I said isn't quite right. It's true I hadn't told Audo straight out, but I think he already realized something was going on."

Thondup's voice came from the bathroom:

"I don't doubt it. It might have been the first cosmogroup he was training, but he had been an instructor before, so he must have been well aware of those love affairs between female pupils and teachers..."

"You're wrong to look at it like that, Thondup. This was something different, and he knew it, although perhaps not during that first year

... but afterwards, yes."

"Just how was it different, if I may ask?"

"In that it was real love."

"Gema ... they all say the same thing."

"You can have your doubts, if you wish; you don't know what it was like."

Thondup came out of the bathroom drying his face. His voice sounded intrigued:

"By the way, nothing showed up in your controls. How was that possible?"

"He fixed them."

Laying down the towel, Thondup stared at her in disbelief:

"That's impossible. Only a specialist, and a very good one at that, could do that and get away with it."

"He was one, Thondup. He had been a team leader at the Suggestology Institute in Tokyo."

"So how come he became a simple instructor? No, Gema, I can't believe it ..."

"You have the proof—look at my control reports."

Thondup carefully edged his way back into bed.

"That may be true ... but I still don't entirely believe you, Gema. I know how intensely you loved—and still love—Isanusi, and I can't reconcile that with the question of your love for Audo."

"Thondup, human beings are more complex than psychosociologists believe ... At least, that's what Audo told me."

"He said that?" He looked at Gema out of the corner of his eye. "It's true then that he was a good psychosociologist."

Gema's eyelids closed, and she heard nothing more.

Audo's hand ruffled her hair, and Gema slowly opened her eyes.

"It's very late, Gema."

With an impulsive movement, Gema held Audo in a tight embrace. A minute later, she pulled away from him. Lying back in the bed, she gazed at him thoughtfully, and he asked,

"Is there something on my face?"

Gema smiled.

"No, nothing." She stretched out her hand and brushed Audo's smiling lips. "It's just that I find it impossible to understand why you haven't been married before …" She could feel his lips tensing beneath her fingers. Immediately curious, she insisted, "So, are you married?"

"I was."

"I'm sorry, my love …"

"No, there's nothing for you to be sorry about … It's an old, silly story. Would you like to hear it?"

"If you really want to tell it."

Audo's eyes strayed from her face and looked at nothing in particular.

"It's very short: I thought she loved me, and I was wrong."

Gema shook her head; her hair fell untidily across the bed.

"You've said too much, or not enough."

"You could be right, my love." Audo sat up in bed, feeling for his clothes. He went on: "She apparently loved me a lot … and I believed her. We lived happily in our little love nest, as she liked to call it, buying furniture, more furniture, and ornaments, lots of ornaments. On weekends, endless parties with other members of the Institute, and long outings in our two-seater levitator. Then one day I asked myself who she really loved: Audo, or the leader of the team."

By now he had finished dressing. He walked across the room, with Gema's attentive eyes on him.

"That might have been nonsense, but I wanted to put it to the test, so I quit my post at the Institute and became an instructor in an out-of-the-way village… in the place where I was born, to be exact."

"And?"

"As expected, she left me. It was the team leader she loved."

"Audo, was it worth doing all that… taking it to that extreme?"

The instructor fixed his gaze on her.

"Of course it was. If only because I got to know you…"

Gema smiled.

"Now I know why you hate Neanderthals so much."

"Nothing better for that than living with one of them, believing them to be a person, until one fine day… Come on, get dressed; the others must be wondering where you are."

Gema obediently got out of bed and started putting on her clothes. Halfway through, she paused, and asked,

"Audo, don't you think the time has come to tell them… about us?"

He took a deep breath.

"I'm afraid that moment will never arrive, Gema."

She stared at him wide-eyed.

"What do you mean?"

"We need to talk; sit down and listen to me."

Gema obeyed mechanically.

"I've been studying your psychoprofile… and that of the others in the group while I was at it. And I can't hold out any hope, Gema."

She murmured,

"No one in the world can remove you from my heart." She shuddered fearfully. "What are you saying? Only words, and clichés at that; this isn't the way, Gema." She managed to control herself, and continued: "I love you, Audo. I love you, and only you, and I feel, I'm convinced, I'm not making a mistake…"

"I wish it were so… but I can't compete against the computers, Gema. They searched through millions and found Isanusi."

Gema felt her heart stop beating. She answered:

"Isanusi is my friend. Nothing more."

"Are you sure?"

Gema lowered her eyes. When she raised her head again, the room was empty.

Thondup's voice emerged from the lightening darkness:

"…understand him, Gema. If he knew that you in fact loved Isanusi, why embark on the adventure with you?"

"He loved me… I'd almost say he still does, Thondup."

"So why choose the course he did? It was the worst, the most painful for the two of you. He should either have ignored you, or to have fought for your love, rather than giving you up as he did, so easily… It all seems very frivolous to me, Gema."

She nodded.

"I thought the same at first…"

She had knocked gently and timidly on the door; there was no reply. She looked back over her shoulder; no one was there.

She called out softly,

"Open the door, Audo; it's me."

The door stayed shut.

"I saw you go in. Please open up, I have to talk to you."

Hearing what sounded like footsteps inside the room, she raised her voice a little:

"Audo…" She lowered it again to an urgent whisper.

"I just want to talk to you for a moment, a minute; I'll leave as soon as you tell me to…"

The future Gema shuddered. "What is this?" She could feel intense waves of pain coming from the other side of the door.

"Open up, Audo; please."

The emotional current flow from inside the room grew more and more intense, until it was practically unbearable…

"He's hesitating, he can't hold out any longer. Insist, Gema, insist." But the Gema from the past had not insisted. She had slowly walked away.

"But in the end I understood Audo and his motives; he took the right course of action."

"He made you suffer, Gema."

"Not very much; Isanusi was there." Noting the expression on Thondup's face, she shook her head. "You still don't see it, do you? Anyone, any of you three or Audo, if you had met any of us three girls in the normal world, would have understood in less than five minutes that she or he were the only one and would have clung to each other. You and Kay, or me and Pavel… Any of us. But in the Academy we were all thrown together. Of course, the psychosociologists already knew what the perfect combinations were: Pavel and Kay, you and Alix, Isanusi and me… but they didn't tell us. They didn't want to influence us, they wanted us to reach the inevitable conclusion on our own, without it seeming forced on us, predetermined by them… In fact, there was no need for them to say anything. There was no way we could fight it. And Audo knew that."

"In that case, he shouldn't have made you fall in love…"

"It was me who made him fall in love, Thondup."

He screwed up his mouth in the darkness.

"It seems to me he was simply taking advantage of the situation."

"You're prejudging him. Kay was very interested in him before I was. It was only after she was convinced he wanted nothing to do with her that she turned to Pavel... No, Audo wasn't like that. Or do you think if he was, they would have allowed him to join the Academy?"

"So what does his romance with you mean?"

"It means he was not a machine, Thondup. He loved me, and gave me what he could. A beautiful, lovely, unforgettable first love... I owe him a lot; he taught me that there is something more than a body and instincts in the relationship between a man and a woman."

"Well, if you say so..."

This time, Thondup's eyes were fixed on Gema's face, and he could see her eyes glaze over.

Standing in front of the mirror, her mouth twisted in a grimace, Gema was contemplating her reflection. From the bed, Alix inquired curiously,

"What are you looking at?"

Still staring at the mirror, Gema replied, "I hate the way I look..."

Alix's eyes were wide open now. Gema went on:

"Oh yes, you've always told me I'm the prettiest in the group... Pretty? I'm like a young, healthy animal, that's all." She held the towel up vertically, covering the bottom half of her body down to her ankles.

"Like this is okay, even if..." She went closer to the mirror until her taut, hard nipples brushed against it, and the vapor from her breath condensed on the cold surface, concealing her face behind a misty veil... She took a step back, and her light-colored eyes reappeared; her lips were still hidden in the wet patch. Still holding the towel, she moved her narrow shoulders, her slender arms, the svelte, flexible torso. She said, as if to herself, "The mouth is too much. The rest is fine; everything normal, nothing exaggerated." She raised her bust. "The breasts as well; they're neither too big nor too small... But the rest..."

She took a step to the side, and let the towel fall. "That's what ruins it all, Alix; one glance at my whole body, and any man can see I'm a female expressly designed to awaken the sexual instinct, and nothing else..." She pointed her chin towards the bathroom, from where they could hear the sound of running water. "If I were like Kay ..." She looked over thoughtfully at the blonde girl sitting on the bed and added, "...or like you; your body is a support, a help, a means of expressing your soul, rather than a bio-organism crying out to all and sundry how perfect it is for sex..." She turned her back on the mirror. "Alix, it makes me furious the way men look at me."

"You used to like it."

"Back then I didn't know..." Breathing heavily, she collapsed on to her bed. She repeated, "There was so much I didn't know..." A lost look appeared on her face as she glanced across at the blonde girl: "Alix, I'm worried that Isanusi only..." She swallowed hard. "I want him to love me for what I am, not just for this." She slid her fingertips down the smooth skin of her thighs. "Do you understand?"

Elbows on knees, hands cupping her face, Alix was observing her.

"You didn't worry like this with Audo."

Gema shrugged.

"That was different."

Alix's nose wrinkled in disapproval.

"So that wasn't serious?"

Gema turned sharply towards Alix, but in the end did not respond. Instead she said,

"You're not entirely mistaken… At least, not at first. But later it was different; Audo didn't love me just for that. In fact, he helped me see it wasn't everything."

Alix stood up and walked over to Gema's bed. She sat near the top, and placed a hand on the naked girl's shoulder. She whispered,

"Well then, in a way he's the one to blame for the way you feel, because he taught you what love is… Don't you think?"

Gema nodded. The tears rolled silently down her face.

Thondup looked concerned. He inquired:

"Gema, how often did you induct yourself during this conversation?"

She held up three fingers.

"Three times?"

"Yes," she replied in a hoarse whisper.

Thondup frowned deeply.

"That's dangerous, Gema, very dangerous. The conditioning may have given you a greater resistance than normal, but it's not infinite. Promise me you won't do it more than three times a day."

"But… but I'm getting results, Thondup."

He looked at her in surprise.

"Results? What kind of results?"

"I managed to perceive an emotional flow… from Audo."

"Are you sure?"

"Sure."

The psychosociologist bit his lips thoughtfully.

"Alright, just as long as you're aware that by doing it so often you might get exhausted, and you could even lose some of what you've already achieved."

"I understand."

He brought his face up to hers.

"And above all, don't induct yourself if I'm not there; that really is dangerous. You remember what happened to me, don't you?"

"I remember."

"Sleep now. I imagine you must be very tired."

"You're not wrong…"

Gema closed her eyes. Thondup waited until her breathing became deep and regular, and only then did he shut his own.

The rustling in the undergrowth grew closer… then Thondup's perspiring face appeared. He blinked in the bright light of the clearing and smiled when he saw them. He said,

"So there you are!" He pushed his way through the remaining branches clinging to his clothes and skin. "I needed to see you, Isanusi."

Isanusi raised himself on one elbow, looking inquiringly at the newcomer striding towards the trees where he and Gema were lying. Sitting down next to them, he declared,

"My cyber's going crazy… And I still don't understand multidimensional transitions. Do you think you can help me?"

Isanusi rolled his eyes.

"Haven't you seen Audo?"

"Audo? Of course…" Thondup scratched the back of his neck, embarrassed. "I saw him and told him about it. He stared at me in that stern way of his and asked me if I thought he looked like a cyberpedagogue."

Gema could not help smiling at this. Isanusi managed to remain serious, although the corners of his mouth twitched. He commented,

"I think he was right, Thondup; we're not back in our precosmic classes now."

"Oh, I'm well aware of that. And yet I still can't understand those transitions..."

He left the sentence incomplete, and Isanusi finished his thought for him:

"So you want to see if my explanations can help, is that it?"

Thondup nodded vigorously.

"Alright. Let's imagine a homogenous bidimensional space..."

Thondup waved his arms:

"Which we then transform into a unidimensional one... No, Isanusi, that's not going to get us anywhere. I know that example by heart, but it doesn't help me understand... My difficulties start when the dimensions are multiplied beyond the common ones..."

"I see... Alright, so let's take a heterogenous pentadimensional space..." He broke off, and looked around. "Where are you going, Gema?"

Without stopping, she answered,

"For a walk, while you explain to Thondup. I'll be back soon."

Isanusi looked at her sympathetically and nodded. Gema pushed her way through the undergrowth... "I'm sorry, but I have enough with my own cyber." She peered among the branches, looking for something. "I thought Kay was coming in this direction. Where can she have got to?" she walked on through tall grasses that covered her bare legs with moisture. She soon came out into another clearing, and saw her companion's familiar figure sitting on the ground. "There she is, but what is she doing?" She approached her slowly, noting the look of concentration on Kay's face as she stared at something she herself could not see. Touching her on the shoulder, Gema asked,

"What are you looking at?"

Kay blinked. Her eyes rose and focused on Gema's face.

"Oh, it's you …" she murmured, and then turned her gaze back to what she had been staring at. "Sit here and look as well. You can't see it standing up."

Gema sat beside her and looked.

"I still don't see anything, Kay."

"The breeze is blowing at the moment, and a branch is casting its shadow, so you'll have to wait … Now!"

A ray of sunlight pierced the shadows. It picked out the intricate design of a spider's web in mid-air. Kay said hastily,

"It's almost finished. It's a shame you didn't come earlier."

A dark blob crawled over the shiny threads. The web grew behind it.

"It's big, isn't it?"

Turning away from the web, Gema gazed at the girl beside her. She murmured thoughtfully,

"How you've changed, Kay…"

Kay turned towards her, her chin jutting defiantly: "So what? Was I obliged to always be the same? That's very boring…" Her face softened, and she asked: "Haven't you changed as well?"

Gema's only answer was a sigh.

Turning towards the trees, Kay listened as the sound of footsteps grew closer. Crumpling her face expressively, she said,

"I think someone is coming who hasn't changed a bit and is never likely to."

Two figures burst into the clearing close to where the spider was spinning its web. The one behind was almost treading on the heels of the person in front… Erik came to a halt, panting, in front of Kay, shaking the remains of the cobweb from his shoulder. A moment later, Pavel was alongside him, talking in short bursts:

"You beat me again... I need to train more."

Erik muttered absently, to no one in particular:

"It's very late. Rex must be looking for me... See you soon."

He trudged away. Pavel frowned as he watched him disappear among the pines. Then he said, in a puzzled voice,

"I think he's annoyed... but I don't know why."

Kay shook her head with evident irritation: "You're incredibly naive, Pavel. Do you think he hasn't realized you let him win?"

Genuinely surprised, Pavel turned to Kay:

"How did you realize?"

"It's far too obvious, Pavel. Why do you do it?"

"I don't see any harm in it, Alix. He likes coming first, so why deny him that pleasure?"

"And you don't mind being last?"

"At running? What does that mean?" He turned to Gema for support. "I simply enjoy running, but I don't see why it's so important if you come first or last—what do you say, Gema?"

Raising her hands to the skies in mock horror, Kay turned to Gema:

"See what I mean? He'll never, ever change..." She suddenly reached out and grabbed Pavel by the wrists, pulling him violently towards her. Caught unawares, the youngster fell to his knees, almost on top of her. Kay kissed him swiftly on the cheek, then moved back. Pavel stared at her, completely at a loss. He protested:

"Gema, can you understand her? One moment she scolds you, almost insults you, then all of a sudden..." He quickly brought his face close to Kay's and returned her kiss before she had time to avoid him. He smiled and went on: "...all of a sudden, something like this. Who can understand her?"

Grasping his waist, Kay responded, eyes shining:

"What are you complaining about? Do you really need to understand me? Isn't it enough to... ?" She did not finish her sentence but looked across at Gema, who rose to her feet slowly and muttered,

"Alright, alright... I can at least understand when I'm not wanted."

Flushing, Kay started to object, but then she saw Pavel's look and desisted. Trying to conceal her confusion, she asked,

"Where is Isanusi?"

Gema pointed to somewhere behind her back.

"Over there... explaining transformations to Thondup."

Pavel and Kay stared at each other, then burst out laughing.

Taken aback, Gema looked at them in astonishment... Pavel was the first to recover his composure sufficiently to explain:

"I think that makes two of us who'll never be analysts. I can't follow transformations either, Gema."

Kay butted in mockingly:

"That's a terrible blow for much vaunted masculine superiority; we girls can do transformations all day long, whereas two out of three boys are still in the dark."

Pavel replied without bitterness:

"But the one male who does understand them can run rings around the girls. Isanusi fully deserves his name, Kay."

Gema asked,

"What name? I don't know what you mean..."

Pavel and Kay smiled. Kay explained:

"It's his own name: Isanusi. Audo told us that in the ancient tongue it comes from, it means "the seer" or "he who sees most." "

Obviously reluctant, Gema accepted their explanation.:

"He must know that then..."

Kay waved her arm.

"Of course he does, but he's too modest, Gema."

"Possibly…" Gema turned on her heel and headed back into the trees. She stopped and added over her shoulder: "At any rate, I'd better go and ask him; I'm still convinced I'm not wanted here."

Snapping twigs and breaking off leaves, Gema pushed her way through the bushes. Not far from her, something rose into the air, too quickly for her to be able to identify it.

Thondup was smiling, amused. He said,

"In the end, I had to go back to my cyber; Isanusi could not work miracles. Anyway, we didn't need six analysts; four were enough."

"Yes, that was enough."

"And when you say we had changed… you were right."

"Yes, a lot."

Thondup scanned her face.

"Don't you feel like talking?"

"No."

"Why? An unpleasant emotional flow?"

"No, not that. Something worse: no flow at all."

Thondup laid a consoling hand on Gema's shoulder.

"Don't worry. The emotional charge isn't always the same; neither is your receptivity. You'll sense them again, sooner or later."

"I hope so…"

Gema frowned unhappily.

"Isanusi, forget you once had vocal chords…" She lowered her voice to an almost normal level. "It is movements of the tongue and the position of your lips – that's what you've got to try to reproduce exactly…" She broke off and corrected herself: "Well, perhaps not exactly, I may not have connected everything perfectly… Try again."

Confused sounds came out of the control panel.

"A-a-a-a-a ..."

Gema nodded, with evident satisfaction.

"That 'A' is much better." Glancing up at the figures on the wall dials, she frowned once more. My hour of work is over, I have to leave you. But take advantage of the next three hours to practice; it's only by constant practice that you'll achieve results, my love... Speaking is not as easy as it seems."

Pressing down hard on the armrests, Gema stood up. She walked to the door with uncertain steps... Before she got there, more sounds emerged from the control panel:

"B-b-b-bye..."

"Did you say goodbye?"

The red light flashed. Gema smiled:

"Thank you, Isanusi..."

She left the bridge. Crossing the lab, she began to walk slowly and deliberately down the poorly-lit corridor. When she opened the cabin door, Thondup greeted her from the bed:

"You took your time, Gema."

She undressed as she moved towards the bed. She apologized:

"I'm sorry, I got caught up in work. Isanusi is making rapid progress; tomorrow he might be able to speak comprehensibly." She lay down in the bed, relaxing her weary body, and asked, "Thondup, why was there no mention of it in the Academy?"

He looked at her blankly.

"Mention of what?"

"This emotional telepathy or whatever it's called. Although the experiment that the twin experts carried out did not succeed, the theory behind it must have appealed to the psychosociologists in the Academy. It's a new and very promising way to strengthen relationships among the members of a group."

"The results of the experiment with the twins were only published shortly before we left, Gema. I saw them by pure chance. Besides, I doubt whether the psychosociologists there are interested in increasing the emotional interdependence between the members of the groups: they're already far too susceptible to loss."

Gema shook her head in disagreement.

"Your reasoning is inconsistent, Thondup. Full emotional communication would increase resistance to any losses. The autonomous units would preserve the dead for the survivors. Besides, I don't see it as simply a protection against any possible deaths. I think that to be able to perceive emotional flows is only a first step towards something qualitatively different... Cosmogroups can be more than what they are now, Thondup."

His lower lip gradually puffed up; he replied laconically:

"This isn't the right moment for speculation, Gema."

The gleam in her eyes died away. She sighed:

"You're right, Thondup." Her voice took on a metallic tone. "I'm going to induct myself, pay attention."

The hatch opened without a sound, and Alix appeared. Her hands were shaking... She saw Gema, and astonishment and terror flashed across her face. She quickly recovered and ran over to her, hugging her and bursting into tears. Gema tried to reassure her:

"Nothing happened, Alix. Look, we're all here."

The blonde girl raised eyes veiled by tears and mumbled,

"But you were dead, Gema... You and Isanusi. Because of me..."

She buried her face in Gema's chest. Clearly annoyed, Thondup turned to Audo:

"Is it necessary to torment her like this?"

The instructor looked at him coldly:

"Would you prefer her to make these mistakes in the real world?"

Thondup licked his lips and replied:

"I just think this amount of realism is exaggerated, Audo. Why don't you use a less convincing simulation? So that we can tell that what's going on isn't for real?"

Audo shook his head.

"The only way to avoid repeating a mistake is to feel the full weight of its consequences."

Alix had regained her composure enough to make peace:

"Audo is right, Thondup. I prefer this to happen to me in the psychosimulator than in reality. If it were real, I couldn't bear it."

Audo asked,

"Who's next?"

Gema stepped forward.

"I am."

The shadows dissolved into the fine lines on Thondup's face.

"Thondup, I succeeded again..."

"Another emotional flow?" Gema nodded, and Thondup questioned her again:

"Who this time?"

"Alix."

Thondup blinked and fell silent. Then he asked, "When was this?"

"Shortly after we began training on the psychosimulators."

"Be more precise, Gema."

"I'm sure you'll remember; it was when Alix killed Isanusi and me for the first time."

Thondup's face showed no emotion.

"Yes, I remember… I protested quite a bit on that occasion, didn't I?" A fleeting smile. "But in the end, those training sessions were useful. Do you know, at first after the collision with the meteorite I thought I was in the psychosimulator." His face darkened. "It took me a while to realize that it was going on for too long, that for this time it was for real… Well, best not relive the bad moments." He looked at the dial on the wall. "It's time for my psychostabilizer."

Turning to one side, he touched the wall, stuck his hand in the cavity that had opened, and took out a pill. Narrowing his eyes, he examined the interior of the drawer. "There aren't many left, Gema." He pushed the pills towards the back of the hole, counting them one by one as he did so. He turned back to face her. "Only enough for three more days."

The boat rocked dangerously… Pavel looked angrily at Kay.

"Don't move, you'll tip us over."

Kay finished pulling her clothes off over her head and explained:

"You can't expect me to stay as still as a statue in this boiling sun when we're surrounded by all this water…"

She put one foot on the side of the boat, pushed off, and dove headfirst into the grey waters of the lake. Isanusi and Gema had to quickly lean over to the opposite side to prevent the boat capsizing. It swayed to and fro, but gradually the rocking subsided… Kay swam towards them with short strokes, smiling broadly.

"Brr, it's cold! Don't you want to come in?"

She splashed water at them. Isanusi and Gema exchanged glances, then also started taking their clothes off… Pavel protested:

"What are you doing? We can't all leave the boat, Isanusi."

Isanusi stood up unsteadily. Scanning the cloudless sky, he replied,

"No sign of a storm, Pavel." He put his clothes under the transom.

Pavel looked from Kay to the other two still in the boat, unable to make up his mind. Isanusi was already standing on the side, about to jump. Gema was standing on the opposite side, ready to act as a balance. Pavel sighed:

"Oh, alright..." He reached for the magnetic clasps on his tunic.

"Nothing this time, Thondup."

Thondup clicked his tongue.

"You can't expect to be successful on every occasion, Gema. Remember we're delving into unexplored territory." Gema did not reply but turned over in the bed, leaving her back towards him.

Closing one eye, Isanusi stared at her. All of a sudden, he turned around and plunged his hands into the clay, muttering,

"I think I've got it this time..."

He picked a spatula off the table and began to use it. The lines became more clear-cut. Gema tiptoed over to the busy sculptor and peered over his shoulder. Isanusi turned his head:

"What are you doing?"

Gema smiled sweetly at him.

"I'm looking at what you're doing, my love. Will it come out alright?"

Isanusi blew out his cheeks in exasperation.

"It'll be more difficult now... you shouldn't have moved, Gema."

"How long did you want me in that position? My muscles ache..."

She gave Isanusi an affectionate kiss behind the ear, then deliberately pressed her body against his back. The spatula wobbled in the novice sculptor's hands.

"Aren't you going to let me finish?"

Gema blew gently on the back of his neck and laughed softly.

"What's got into you now?"

She whispered in his ear:

"You've got goose bumps."

Isanusi raised his eyes to the white ceiling with a sigh.

"I'll never get it done, Gema."

She took the spatula from him and placed it back on the table. Isanusi turned to face her, trying to keep the stern look on his face.

"What are you trying to do?"

Gema gazed at him affectionately.

"I don't know why you're so worried about the copy, when you've got the original right next to you." She sat on his lap, threw her arms around his neck, and whispered:

"Can't you understand how cold I am, without any clothes on?"

Isanusi's eyes opened wide with surprise.

"So sorry for not realizing, madam..."

He wrapped his arms around her waist.

"Well?"

Gema was breathing heavily. She didn't respond to his question. Thondup insisted:

"Did you manage to intercept another emotional flow? Whose was it this time?"

Gema stared at him.

"Thondup, I need to ask you a favor."

"What is it?"

"Go to the cabin Isanusi and I used to share. In the cupboard above the bed you'll find a small clay statue. Bring it for me."

Thondup dragged himself to the door.

"Is this it?"

Gema's eyes opened, and stared at the object. She stretched out her hands and said,

"Yes; give it to me."

Thondup handed it to her. Gema stood it on the bed very carefully, and contemplated it for a long time... Thondup cleared his throat.

"Can you tell me now which episode you revisited?"

"You don't know it. It was when Isanusi was making this."

She felt the golden statue with her fingers, murmuring:

"I don't look like that at all now, do I, Thondup?"

He surveyed her skinny body on the bed before replying non-committedly,

"No, not your body... but the face is still recognizable. Of course, the features stand out more, but..."

"That's enough, Thondup."

Gema was looking down at her concave stomach. She lifted her hand and touched her lower ribs, then her fingertips descended to her smooth flank, rose to her prominent iliac crest, then around the pelvis to her pubic bone, then up again to the sternum... She let her hand drop on to the bed.

"Not an ounce of fat." She raised her forearms and studied them. "My muscles are weakening, going flabby." She cast a critical eye over the man sitting on the bed, and said: "You're in no better shape, Thondup. We've lost our physiological balance; we're losing more than we're taking in. Our intestines obviously cannot properly absorb nourishment. There's nothing else for it, we're going to have to feed ourselves intravenously..."

Pavel removed the video-reader and put it away, complaining,

"I don't know why you recommended it, Audo. I didn't like it at all."

Alix turned her head towards him.

"What were you reading, Pavel?"

"Annoyán's memoirs."

Audo had finished stuffing his pipe. He lit it and puffed at it with evident satisfaction. He asked,

"What is it you don't like about them, Pavel?"

The youngster shrugged hesitantly.

"I don't know... Perhaps it's the way he behaves at difficult moments. Of course, I realize that they were really difficult and that most of the time he behaved correctly, but his way of reacting seemed to me too melodramatic..." He waved his hands, trying to find the right words: "I can't explain, but it I think it's an over-exaggeration."

Isanusi spoke up from the far end of the room:

"I know what you mean. I've read the book as well..." He glanced at Audo. "I agree with Pavel. To illustrate what I mean, take the example of a man who shouts out excitedly: "I'm breathing! I'm breathing!" He shook his head. "In my opinion, there's no need to make such a song and dance about doing what is necessary."

Pavel turned enthusiastically to Isanusi.

"Exactly—that was my impression too." He looked at Audo. "Why did he have to act like that? He did the right thing, in most cases..."

Gema murmured, as if to herself,

"He seems so primitive to me... That must have been how the cavemen tribes behaved, leaping and shouting around their bonfire, to encourage in each other the state of mind they wanted to achieve."

Isanusi waved a hand in agreement.

"I think you've got it, Gema: the primitive, almost ancestral character. Their actions don't arise from a deep, sincere conviction, but from emotional urges that are instinctive, deliberately provoked and stimulated...

Thondup twisted his mouth:

"I would never behave like that, Isanusi."

Audo's lively eyes fixed on him:

"Are you sure, Thondup?"

The youngster smiled.

"As far as anyone can be sure..."

Kay was watching them silently, her chin cupped in her hand. Audo addressed her:

"What do you say?"

She looked at him astutely.

"Me? I've got nothing to say; I simply wonder why you recommended the whole group read those memoirs."

Audo did not reply but concentrated on his pipe.

Eyes shining, Isanusi said,

"I can imagine the reason, Kay."

Audo took the pipe out of his mouth:

"You think so?"

"I think so."

"Tell us then..." Audo replaced the pipe.

Isanusi turned to the rest of the group:

"Once upon a time there was an instructor who was very concerned about his group... They seemed to him to be cold, showing little enthusiasm. That made him feel awkward, very awkward. How could he be certain they would be able to face difficult situations? They would need to show enthusiasm, to see the kind of flame that can overcome any obstacle... But how could he achieve that?"

He cast an inquiring glance over their attentive faces and went on:

"The instructor thought it would be a good idea to offer them examples from the past that showed how our ancestors were able to grow when faced with apparently insurmountable difficulties and find a way to overcome them. Yes, there are many such examples from history..."

He looked at Audo out of the corner of his eye. "So that's what he did; but the group's reaction took him by surprise. Whilst they admired the heroes who were forged in those struggles, to his astonishment they were not attracted to their way of doing things..." Isanusi swiveled his chair until he was facing Audo. "Perhaps it's better to forget the legend and talk openly. Audo, we may not be as expressive or emotive as Annoyán, but I don't think that will be an obstacle when it comes to us having to face any difficulties we encounter." He looked over his shoulder. "What do you others say?"

Thondup shifted in his seat and muttered,

"I think that if you are truly convinced of something, there's no need to be shouting about it from the rooftops."

Alix backed him up.

"I'm not convinced by these feverish outpourings either, Audo. They can act both ways, positively or negatively."

Pavel leaned forward in his chair:

"Of course, this doesn't mean we underestimate the past, or the men living back then. They acted within the limits of their possibilities, the ways of behaving of their time. What's really important is that they did what they had to: I don't think we can ask any more of them."

"But we have our own way of behaving, and I don't think that's any worse, Audo," said Kay.

The pipe came out of the instructor's mouth once more.

"What do you say, Gema?"

She raised her eyebrows.

"You'll have to forgive me, but to be frank I don't see why we're talking about this. I would prefer to wait for the problem to arise; then we'd see what we are really capable of.

Everything we say now is ..." She hesitated, searching for the right word: "Unnecessary."

Audo laughed loud and long. Drying his tears, he muttered,

"I'm sorry all of you, but Gema has cut the ground from under you with her dispassionate and so terribly concrete analysis."

Gema blushed and lowered her eyes. Audo become serious again:

"There's no need to feel ashamed, Gema. What you've said is quite right; to a certain extent, we're swimming on dry land."

Turning to Isanusi, he continued:

"Nor were you too wide of the mark with your legend..." He smiled. "You'll all have to forgive me. It's old age, I'm starting to talk nonsense."

Apparently dreadfully upset, Kay replied,

"Oh, I don't think there's anything to be done with us by now, Audo. I'd recommend you speak to Rex. His group is noisy enough to keep you satisfied; you could do a swap..." She raised her hand to wipe away an imaginary tear, then sobbed: "Although we'd really miss you..."

Pavel took her to task:

"That's a poor joke, Kay." He spoke directly to their instructor. "Audo, what confuses me is that you yourself are not very... expressive, to call it something, so I don't see why we have to be."

The instructor agreed:

"You're right, Pavel. As far as I can tell, I've come up against one of the 'fundamentals' of this group. That's one of the dangers of being an instructor; sometimes I worry unnecessarily, like the hen who's hatched duck eggs and is at a loss when they take to the water..."

Smiles all around.

"Audo, how is it you never became a cosmonaut?" asked Thondup.

The instructor carefully tipped the contents of the pipe into the ashtray and answered him:

"I was born too soon, Thondup. I was already twenty when the first precosmic group was formed in my native land... but I still haven't lost all hope of exploring the Cosmos." He smiled when he saw their astonished looks. "Yes, don't be amazed: I think that when you travel out there, you'll be taking part of me with you... and I think that will be the only way my wish is granted."

Gema waved a hand in agreement.

"Yes, I did sense several emotional flows, but I'm not sure I assimilated them very well, Thondup. We were all together, so it was hard to tell whom they were coming from... And yet I felt I was perceiving something new: above and beyond individual differences, there was a common thread..."

"That's only logical, Gema: by then, our group had consolidated." Thondup stared down at the thin tube sticking out of the vein in his forearm. "It's coming to an end—how do I get this out?"

"Wait, I'll show you."

She unscrewed the valve between the tube and his arm. The transparent length fell away, leaving the needle in the flesh.

"That's it."

Thondup stared at the blunt end of the needle rising from his skin.

"Aren't you going to remove that as well?"

"No, I don't want to run the risk of a hemorrhage."

Thondup move his arm warily.

"Won't it get in the way when I'm working?"

"Of course not; it's not in any muscle." Rolling up the sleeve of her tunic, Gema showed him her own forearm. "See? I've left mine in. It doesn't get in the way at all."

Thondup carefully rolled down his sleeve, then stood up.

"I'm going to see Isanusi; I need to ask him…"

"Don't go."

Thondup looked at her in surprise.

"Why?"

"He still can't talk to you. Better wait until tomorrow."

"But didn't you tell me he's already talking clearly?"

Gema finished putting away the transfusor in a brusque manner.

"Yes… but only a few words, and he still can't…" Looking straight at Thondup, she said: "Please, do me a favor; wait until tomorrow."

"If that's what you want…"

"It is."

Gema leaned back in her seat, tired but happy.

"We're making progress, Isanusi." She peered at the glowing lights on the wall. "We still have some time left; we can talk." She paused. Her hands fluttered restlessly, unable to find anywhere to rest. "I wanted to ask you…" She fell silent again. She took a deep breath and made her mind up: "Have you managed to perceive anything during your eidetic states?"

"Y-yes."

Gema beamed.

"You have? Me too." She leaned over the monitor and continued in a low whisper. "I also wanted to tell you… that occasionally, at certain moments, I've managed to sense what you were feeling." An intake of breath. "And you… have you been able to receive any of what I…" She left her question unfinished and waited with bated breath.

"Y-yes."

Gema's cheeks flushed. Smiling, she stroked the edge of the panel softly, very softly... Then she saw the dial, and frowned:

"We've run out of time, Isanusi; I have to go."

As she struggled to her feet, from the panel came, clearly:

"S-see you so-on, Gema."

"See you soon, my love."

One of Erik's eyes narrowed, while the eyebrow of the other lifted:

"Four analysts? In a group of only six? That's far too many."

Isanusi shrugged slightly and answered:

"That depends what for... That combination is used a lot for explorations."

Erik smiled wryly.

"Explorations? I'm afraid this isn't a good time for them, Isanusi." He pointed to the stars beyond the glass wall. "They're just finishing exploring the moons of Jupiter. By the time it's our turn it will be the gap between Jupiter and Saturn, without any Asteroid Belt to compensate for it. It will be quite a few years before we have ships capable of crossing that abyss. No, now it's time to consolidate what has already been achieved. Lots of groups will be needed for the Orbital City, for the bases researching the asteroids and Jupiter, for Venus and Mars, and for the expansion of the mining and energy operations on the Moon. But not for exploration. All those areas need specialists: planetary experts, scientists, cyberneticists. Topnotch researchers... not analysts."

From the couch, Tania struck a conciliatory note:

"The two things aren't incompatible, Erik. If necessary, an analyst can specialize. Besides, don't forget we all have a second profession..."

Erik dismissed her argument out of hand:

"Yes, we all have a second profession, Tania, but the problem lies in the training itself, in the general scope of what analysts learn...

Like it or not, they can't go as deeply into a subject as specialists do."

"But they have an important role to play in interdisciplinary groups, Erik." Tania glanced at Isanusi and Gema as though apologizing, before continuing: "They're always needed..."

"Of course. But in what ratio? Two or at most three in a group of eight or ten." Annoyed, Erik stared at Tania: "I don't know why you're so keen to defend them. After all, you're not an analyst either."

Tania's eyes glinted.

"No, I'm not, and nor are you. But they are."

Erik looked at Gema and Isanusi over his shoulder.

"Yes, I know that. They could have said exactly what you said, but you chose to speak for them and not let them in the conversation."

Tania was exasperated:

"Erik, you ought to realize that as a simple question of tact, of courtesy, you shouldn't have said what you did."

"Why? We've known them for years, Tania... I don't think I've offended or upset them, if that's what you're worried about. You know we've always liked to discuss things."

Gema was quick to respond, before Tania could do so:

"It's true, Taniusha, we really don't feel in the last bit offended." She looked across beseechingly at Isanusi. "Isn't that right?"

Isanusi said with a smile,

"Absolutely right."

A door opened, and Pavel and Kay entered.

"Sorry we're late, but Kay decided to change at the last minute." Pavel scanned Gema and Isanusi's faces. He went on, concern in his voice: "I hope you weren't bored."

"Not at all, Pavel; we were chatting," Isanusi reassured him, still smiling. Gema looked curiously at the strange contraption.

"What's this, Thondup?"

He touched the control panel, and the two transporters rose into the air with a faint hum, linked by a metal bar.

"So that we can move around the ship without getting so tired, Gema." He walked over and stood between the two transporters. Placing his arms on top of the metal bar, he was able to reach the controls. "See?" He pressed a button, and the transporters glided forward with a gentle purr. Suspended between them, Thondup was able to walk quickly. "Since you say we can't reduce the gravity field any further…" He stopped, pressing another button.

Gema shook her head.

"No, Thondup, less than 0.4G is not safe in our condition."

"Then let's use this." He patted the dark top of the transporter, then looked at her. "Shall I make one for you?"

"Alright."

The sand was scorching: turning onto her back, Gema surveyed their surroundings, in search of shade… Her eyes fell on the nearby palm trees.

"Isanusi, shall we move over there?"

He raised his head.

"Where?"

Gema pointed:

"Over there, under the palm trees."

Shading his eyes with his hand, Isanusi observed how low the sun was in the sky.

"It's getting late, Gema. We'd better have a last dip in the lake to wash off the sand…"

Isanusi broke off so suddenly that Gema glanced across at him. He was staring at something behind them. She asked automatically,

"What are you looking at?" Without awaiting his reply, she also turned around to look. Dazzled by the gleaming sand, she found it hard to focus properly. As she was doing so, Isanusi answered:

"Someone's coming… and they seem to be in a great hurry."

Screwing up her eyes, Gema finally spotted the figure moving towards them. She said, "It looks like… No; it's Thondup." She turned her head to her companion: "What can be going on?"

Isanusi shrugged his shoulders.

"I've no idea… We'd better go and meet him, Gema."

They walked across the thin strip of sand at the water's edge… Thondup had collapsed on the ground. He waited, panting, for them to reach him. He waved his hand in greeting, and said in a rush,

"The expedition… Ganymede: they're not answering…"

The Pioneers' Promenade was filled with a dense mass of people talking as they walked along, looking up helplessly at the blue, cloudless sky… The three of them managed to push their way through to the rest of the group surrounding Audo.

Isanusi asked, "What do you know for sure, Audo?"

Their instructor shot them a worried look.

"Not a lot. They were supposed to get in touch today, at noon. We're still trying to establish contact with them…"

"Haven't they asked the bases on the Asteroid Belt for information? Perhaps they received something…"

"Yes, we've been in touch with them; they know nothing."

Gema began to cry silently. Isanusi put an arm around her:

"Gema, we don't know anything definite yet. It could just be that their transmitter is broken…"

Gema nodded but went on sobbing. As if from far off in the distance, she heard Audo's dry voice:

"Your rest period is over; it's time to get back to work."

"Tell me what you can see, Isanusi."

It was some time before the reply came from the panel.

"Stars … and the sun. Strange, the glare doesn't bother me, Gema."

"I added a brightness filter to your optic nerves; I'm glad it's working." She turned a knob to the right.

"I can't see anything now, Gema."

"That's because I've disconnected the visualizer. We have other things to do now, Isanusi."

"Does that mean I have to be blind again?"

"I promise that as soon as we've finished I'll connect your vision. Let's get to work: I've made some direct connections between your brain and the auxiliary memories and the ultra-rapid calculation centers. Let's see if they are working too… Tell me, what's the 11th root of 1,977,326,743?"

She barely had a chance to say the last number before the monitor answered:

"Seven."

"Correct." Gema adjusted some controls and said: "This time, don't speak; just think of the answer. What's the hyperbolic sine of 1.443 raised to the 5th power, divided by the 8th root of the factorial of 18?"

The figures immediately flashed up on the screen.

Gema smiled.

"You're working perfectly, Isanusi."

"What happened?"

"You gave the answer on the screen. Right again; you're not making any mistakes…"

"It's the ultra-rapid calculator, not me, Gema."

"Why not? It's part of you now." She changed the position of a relay and said, "Now answer out loud, Isanusi…"

She typed several buttons on the control panel quickly.

"12.7888..." Isanusi responded. "What did you do? I could sense the input but not hear it."

"I sent them by typing on the controls. Wait a moment..." Gema leaned forward and took a dozen cards from inside the computer. She slotted them on to the input tray for the main panel.

"Here are the control questions; they'll take you longer. You can do them while I'm resting; three hours should be more than enough. See you then, Isanusi..."

"Haven't you forgotten something?"

Gema turned a knob back to the left.

"As you can see, I didn't forget."

"Thanks... By the way, wouldn't it be possible to connect my optic nerves to the intercom? I'd like to be able to see you two again..."

"Later, Isanusi. For now we have to concentrate on the fundamental task: to prepare you to pilot the ship."

"Yes, you're right. But you can't imagine how I long to see you and Thondup, again."

Gema gave a strained smile.

"I don't recommend it. Neither Thondup nor I are a sight worth seeing, my love." Without waiting for his reply, she started up the transporters, which slowly rose to chest level. She thrust her arms over the linking bar, worked the controls, and the machine rose in the air once more, helping her to her feet. She signed off:

"Goodbye for now, Isanusi."

"Bye for now, Gema."

Curving through the air, the transporters took her to the door.

Her elbows on the windowsill, Gema let out a sigh. Kay immediately looked up from her video-reader.

"Are they coming?"

Gema turned to her: "No, I can't see them yet."

"Well then? Why such a deep sigh?"

"I was thinking about the international situation."

Kay made a face.

"Couldn't you think about anything more interesting?"

Alix sat up on the couch and muttered offhandedly:

"Be quiet, silly; it's not something for you to joke about."

Kay looked from one to the other.

"I only hope the boys finish their tests soon... Since they've been gone, you two have been unbearably serious, deadly dull. There's no putting up with you."

With that, she disappeared into her room. Gema watched her go:

"How she misses Pavel."

"She doesn't miss him, Gema. She can't; they just left six hours ago. No, she's worried about them; she's afraid they won't pass."

"We did, didn't we?"

"But it wasn't that easy, if you remember. Of course, I'm not concerned for Isanusi, but Thondup and Pavel..."

Alix did not finish; her face was solemn.

Gema said,

"It's a shame they split our group up, out of all the ones there are. If that female examiner had been better prepared, we could have all finished together."

"It didn't depend on her, Gema. What happened was that there weren't sufficient individual booths."

"I know, Alix. And it was real torture: what a way to probe our weak points... I felt morally naked in front of her. She's really sly."

"Don't blame her so much; the perverse ones are those who programmed her."

"They say she can program herself…"

"That's no more than a student myth, Gema; the terror she causes could lead to far worse fantasies. I myself have heard that she immediately knows, wherever she may be, when somebody has failed a test." Getting up from the couch, Alix went on: "Why don't we talk about something else. For example, the international situation you're so worried about?"

Gema nodded docilely.

"As you wish…" She made an effort to remember. "I was thinking how expensive the Empire is for us. Can you imagine how many millions the Federation has to spend?"

"No, I can't: tell me."

"I don't know the exact figure either, but I can imagine it must be astronomical. And when I think that the day the Empire no longer exists, all that money could be spent on investigating the Cosmos… It would be so wonderful to live to see it, Alix."

Kay's head appeared in the doorway.

"I wouldn't be so sure, Gema." She came out of her room and walked over to the two other girls. "All those funds will be needed to develop the marginal areas of the Empire. And it could well be they will have to find more money and take that from what's been assigned to the Cosmos. As they say, every silver lining has a cloud."

"If you put it that way, then they would be justified in spending the money on that, Kay. Although I reckon the Empire has more than enough funds itself," said Gema.

Alix did not agree.

"I think Kay is right on this, Gema. Rebuilding the Empire's economy is going to cost us… although of course, it will be worth it."

Kay laughed out loud.

"You two are very quick to bury the Empire... It's a shame it shows no sign of granting your wish." Her face took on a mischievous look, and she whispered: "I know, I know when the monster will fall..."

Alix asked her with a smile,

"When?"

Before replying, Kay sat on the couch next to Alix:

"I'll tell you, if you promise not to laugh; I'm being serious."

Slightly incredulous, Gema promised:

"I won't laugh, Kay."

"And you, Alix?"

"I can't make that kind of promise where you're concerned, Kay."

"Mock away, it doesn't matter..." She lowered her voice. "I was born the day the Empire was created. When my grandmother heard the news, she prophesied—she's a bit of a witch, you know?—she prophesied that the Empire, born on the same day as me, would perish on the same day as well. And my mom told her that if that was the case, she wouldn't mind the Empire lasting a thousand years."

As she spoke, Alix's eyebrows had knitted into a frown.

"Now I see where your irreverent nature comes from... all from your mother's side."

"What would you have preferred? For my mother to strangle me in my cot, to speed up the end of the Empire?"

Gema intervened, trying to suppress a laugh:

"I don't know why, but it seems Alix wouldn't have minded that too much..."

"But fortunately, good old maternal instinct won out, so you'll have to put up with me."

Alix shrugged her shoulders, smiling.

"It's not such a huge punishment, Kay; you could be worse."

"Praise indeed!"

Gema was curious:

"Why don't you tell us more about your grandmother, Kay?"

Alix had stretched out on her stomach on the couch once more. Her eyes gleaming ironically, she said,

"Why do you ask her that? Are you interested in witches and black magic?" She looked across at Kay: "From everything she's said, her native region must be incredibly primitive. I can see it now: a dusty town, full of churches, monasteries, convents..."

Gema pretended she was playing a flute and added,

"With snake-charmers, mysterious fakirs and head-hunters."

Kay wrapped an imaginary cloak around herself:

"How dare thee, heretics, make fun of all that is holy?" She looked daggers at them. "No matter. God will punish thee, not in this world, where Satan holds sway, but in the next. Heed the sacred voice that warns thee: Beware the eternal flames of hell..."

Alix crawled off the couch and kneeled beseechingly at Kay's feet: "Forgive us, oh divine Sibyl; our ignorance has led us into sin. Save us, show us the way to the Cosmos... I mean, the heavens."

Kay adopted a cavernous tone:

"It would be better for you not to set your sights so high... It demands far too great a sacrifice for your sinner's flesh, O wretched mortal. You will have to do battle all alone against the terrible monster, the snake of a thousand heads, the federal examiner. If you vanquish her, then you will be able to ascend at least to the Orbital City."

Gema was doubled up laughing. Alix was wondering what to reply, when a disgruntled voice reached them from the doorway:

"D'you see this, Audo? And you were saying the girls were wasting away with sadness..." Isanusi shook his head dolefully. "We shouldn't have been in such a hurry to tell them the result of our test."

Hearing Isanusi's voice, Alix leapt up out of her seat, anxiously scanning the faces of the new arrivals. Then she shouted joyfully:

"They passed!" She turned, beaming, towards Gema and Kay. "They passed; they vanquished the thousand-headed snake!"

Kay had already run across and thrown herself into Pavel's arms. Her eyes were moist as she whispered,

"You've no idea how worried I was, my love."

"Yes we do; we've been watching for a while through the glass wall." He winked at her.

"I was genuinely annoyed, Gema," said Thondup. "We didn't get up to tricks like that to relieve the tension while you girls were being tested."

"That's because you didn't have Kay with you."

"That's quite likely," the psychosociologist admitted, still looking impatiently at the slow speed the liquid was descending in his transfusor. "Kay was incorrigible."

"She wasn't that bad," Gema retorted. "When the situation demanded, she showed her courage. Not even a cyber could have been cooler or more analytical... Or have you forgotten when the explorer vehicle got stuck in the launch bay? Kay more than demonstrated what she was worth on Titan."

"That's true," Thondup agreed. Stretching out his hand to the valve, he sighed with relief: "Finished." He extracted the tube from the needle sticking in his forearm and sat up, leaning on one elbow. He immediately fell back, murmuring, "I'd better rest a little longer."

"Don't worry; there are still a few minutes," said Gema. She switched on her transporters, and the apparatus slowly moved off.

"So why are you leaving, Gema?"

"I have to..."

A sudden thrust of *Sviatagor*'s engines made her lose her balance. She let go of the transporters and stumbled, hitting the wall and sinking in to the soft layer of polyfoam. She slipped down it until she was seated on the floor. Thondup asked from his pod,

"Have you hurt yourself?"

"No." Gema reached out to the wall to try to stand up but slid to the ground once more. She asked in an urgent voice,

"Give me a hand, Thondup; I need to make use of this new change."

"To do what?" he asked, but she did not reply. He climbed out of his pod and used his transporters to help him over to Gema's apparatus, which was spinning slowly in mid-air. He took it to her, and she grasped it to haul herself to her feet. She said,

"Come with me; I'll probably need your help."

The transporters carried them at top speed along the corridor. They slowed up to cross the lab and came to a halt on the bridge, opposite Isanusi. Gema sat in the pilot's seat and indicated for Thondup to sit beside her:

"Sit here." She glanced at the monitor. "Isanusi, pay attention to the data I'm going to input..." Staring at the fluctuating figures on the dials, she nimbly entered figures on the keyboard for a few seconds, then sighed: "That's everything."

Isanusi asked,

"What time shall I set the correction of the trajectory for?"

"In forty-five minutes."

Intrigued, Thondup glanced at her:

"Why so long, Gema? You only need ten minutes to calculate..."

"And Isanusi needs much less. But it's not a question of simply calculating it, Thondup." She glanced at the control panel. "Finished, Isanusi?"

"Yes, look at the screen."

The numbers flashed up in sequence, appearing and disappearing in fractions of a second… Thondup complained:

"I didn't see a thing, Gema."

"I did…" She relaxed in her seat, a broad smile on her face. "I'm beginning to think you'll reach Earth, Isanusi!" She turned to Thondup: "Can you reconnect Palas to the engines in half an hour?" Scratching his head, Thondup replied,

"I can try…"

Propelled by his transporters, Thondup left the bridge. Settling in her seat, Gema said,

"Another check is always good, Isanusi: can you repeat it for me?"

The control panel announced:

"For the first engine, say clearly to myself: 'first engine,' while at the same time flexing the index finger on my left hand. When the connection is established, think of the parameters for its functioning: in the first place, the angle of ejection of the thrust nozzle. Second, total mass to be ejected. Third, the equation for the variation of the intensity of propellant flow as a function of time. Fourthly, the time difference between giving the order and when the engine has to start up… For the second engine, say clearly to myself 'second engine' and at the same time, pull the abductor muscles of my right hand…"

The raindrops beat rhythmically against the glass. The pines became confused shadows that were clear, then blurred, as the rain trickled down the smooth, cold surface.

"Hypnotized by the rain, Gema?"

She shivered slightly. Without looking around, she replied,

"No. On the day I arrived it was raining just like this…"

Raising her eyes from the video-reader, Alix glanced at the glass wall and agreed:

"It's true, it was a light drizzle, exactly like this."

Gema turned away from the pane.

"Why can they have called Isanusi?"

Thondup said, half-smiling:

"To check we haven't escaped, out of boredom…"

"Most likely they've only just remembered us, Thondup. Someone must have found the mislaid document and, eyes opening wide, said, 'Look at this! We've still got one group left.' Somebody else must have replied, 'What a shame they've turned up now, when there's nothing left to do.' And the first one, still staring in astonishment at the piece of paper, probably asked, 'What can we do with them?' The second man, with a yawn, advised him, 'Don't get worked up, old man. Find them and tell them they'll have to wait for next year's projects. They're young, they'll have more than enough…'"

Kay was unable to continue because a strong hand covered her mouth. She looked up at Pavel, who explained:

"It's just in self-defense, Kay. If I hear any more of this story, I'll have to run away."

The visible part of the girl's face gazed at him entreatingly.

"Alright, if you promise to behave…"

Kay blinked in agreement, and Pavel withdrew his hand.

"So now what do we do?" Alix asked the ceiling; but that was not where the reply came from.

"Start training…"

Every head turned towards the door of the elevator. Isanusi was smiling at them. He announced, with restrained satisfaction,

"We've been given a mission, all of you; a good mission."

"…maintenance of the internal conditions onboard ship."

"That's easier. All that's needed are the protocols stored in the auxiliary memories..."

"What happens if there's a breakdown?"

"Thondup has disconnected all the equipment not strictly necessary for the ship to reach Earth, and he's busy installing backups of all the important systems."

"How will I know an apparatus has stopped working properly?"

"Wait a second..." Gema changed a control. "What do you feel?"

"Cold... on my cheeks."

"That means the temperature on the bridge has dropped too low; in other words, the thermo-control system in here has a malfunction."

"Then what do I do?"

"You activate the duplicate system; that's easy. Let's codify this specific case: malfunction of the thermo-control system on the bridge..." She pressed several buttons and left her finger gently on a switch. "When I say so, think 'Heat Control On' and turn your head to the right. NOW."

She flicked the switch, then closely studied the dials. "Good... Now let's see if it works." Her hands glided over the controls for a moment, then she said, "Repeat the code."

Green lights flashed on the control panel, in no apparent order.

"It works, Isanusi. We can go on to 'Heat Control Two,' which corresponds to the lab."

"Wait, Gema. There's something I have doubts about. These systems, especially the drive, can have backups, because their basic mode of operation is the same. But that's not so for other equipment. If there are problems with any of them, what shall I do?"

"Thondup has checked everything carefully, Isanusi. He's changed or repaired all the parts he wasn't sure about... Besides, we still have a week or two to live; if any breakdowns occur within that time that you can't repair, we'll help you as best we can. Afterwards... I think you can trust *Sviatagor*; I remember that in our entire journey, Palas only had to turn to us three times. I don't believe that in the last three or four weeks of our flight it's going to fail us..."

Pavel touched a corner of the rectangular screen, and the hologram appeared, bursting with life. The figures were only a third life-size, but their features were perfectly distinguishable: Alix's blonde hair seemed to be ruffled by the breeze... Audo was visibly moved.

"Thank you, all of you..." He pointed to the image of Thondup. "You're identical to when I first saw you; it's perfect."

"And that's not all, Audo. Look at this." Pavel turned a small knob, and the people in the hologram slowly transformed: Isanusi grew a couple of inches, Thondup's shoulders broadened, Kay's silhouette filled out; their faces aged.

"What's this?"

"Gema and Kay did it; they've outdone themselves," explained Thondup.

"On the basis of our yearly holograms, they established the changes to our features during the intervening periods."

"Great work... Thank you, thank you very much."

"That isn't all," said Kay. "Give it him, Isanusi."

Isanusi came over, carrying a carved wooden pipe in both hands. He gave it ceremoniously to Audo and insisted,

"You have to try it at once, Audo."

"Well... as you all wish." He took out his tobacco pouch.

They looked at him as he filled and lit the new pipe. Alix asked,

"What's the new group like?"

Their instructor blew out the first mouthful of smoke.

"They seem promising…" A humorous glint appeared in his eyes. "On the very first day, when I'd barely finished talking to them, one of them stood up looking at me suspiciously and snapped, 'I don't know what you can teach us that the cybers can't…'"

They all laughed, and Audo added, "That reminds me of how time passes. When I was his age, I used to ask the opposite question…"

Isanusi threw Thondup a malicious glance:

"I don't think you need look too far for examples like that, Audo…"

Turning around, Thondup stared with astonishment at the broken videophone screen.

"Why did you do that, Gema?"

As she laboriously picked the shiny fragments up from the floor, Gema explained:

"I'm going to connect Isanusi's vision to the intercom, Thondup. He'll need it as he approaches Earth."

He sat on the edge of his pod and let go of the transporters. They drifted silently down to the floor.

"But why break the screen? He won't be able to see us when we're in here, Gema."

"Precisely for that reason… I have to tell you that from now on we won't be leaving here, unless there's a malfunction that Isanusi can't repair; I've just handed control of the ship over to him." As she spoke, Gema had lain down in her pod. She waved in the direction of the transfusor and said: "We have all we need here, Thondup." She gazed around the sick bay and came to a halt on his face. "Our work has finished… our physical work, I mean." She settled in her bed. "And just in time; I have to confess I couldn't do any more."

Thondup looked at her thoughtfully.

"I still don't understand why you smashed the visual channel on the intercom, Gema."

She gently ran a hand through her hair, then showed it to him.

"Perhaps this will satisfy you, Thondup."

She held her hand outside the pod and shook it slightly. Great clumps of hair fell slowly to the floor. She said,

"I think it'll be better for him to keep the image he has of how we used to be... Now, if you don't mind, let's drop it. Thondup, there's something that's worrying Isanusi and me."

"What's that?"

"We've managed to perceive the emotional flows of the group quite clearly and in a regular manner while we've been inducted, and yet we can't establish any direct contact between the two of us in a normal state. We need your advice: What method did the twin experts use in their experiment to achieve direct contact?"

It was some time before Thondup replied:

"Gema, I'm worried about your physical condition. This may be subjective, but it doesn't seem to me that you're in any better state than me, although you had a smaller dose of radiation."

"You're not wrong; the analyses show that the effects of radiation are appearing in me more rapidly than expected. In fact it seems at the moment that I won't live much longer than you; if I'm lucky, a week, no more. But you didn't answer my question, Thondup."

"You answered it yourself, Gema: the effort is killing you."

"A few days more or less don't matter. If I can ensure that Isanusi constructs the autonomous units in his mind, I can die happy."

Thondup twisted his mouth in what seemed almost like a smile.

"I would hate to be left alone here with your dead body, Gema."

"You don't have to worry about that. As soon as the pod confirms I am dead, the lid will close over me. The smell of my decomposition won't bother your pleasure-seeking nose... Anyway, you won't be alone; Isanusi will be there."

Thondup whispered, "Is the audio channel on?"

Gema glanced across at him, then a second later up at the monitor.

"No, it's not connected. Why did you want to know?"

"So that I could tell you that no group of experts on twins ever did that experiment on emotional telepathy."

Gema's eyes narrowed. She asked hoarsely,

"Explain yourself."

"There's not much to explain. In the meeting—do you remember? I applied what you yourself suggested."

"What I suggested?"

"Yes. You wanted me to induct him, or hypnotize him so that he would believe we were still alive, didn't you?"

"But you said that was impossible."

"And I wasn't lying; it was true. And yet your idea was a good one, so I put it into practice. Naturally, I adapted it to the circumstances."

"I don't understand, Thondup."

"But it couldn't be clearer... Listen: given the lack of resources on the ship, it was impossible for me to implant the suggestion in Isanusi's mind that we were still alive in the hibernation pods. I could not erase his knowledge of the deaths of Alix and Pavel, nor what you had just explained about how it would be impossible for us to go into hibernation. Luckily, there was one way out..."

"To suggest he could keep us as autonomous units in his mind?"

"Exactly."

For a long while, Gema said nothing.

"And yet it's true that Sakharov's theory about mental representation is unable to explain the emotional flows between closely-linked people, Thondup."

The psychosociologist waved away her objection:

"Yes, that's true. But nobody has dared to work in that field, Gema; it's full of practical difficulties. How can one distinguish between true and false in such an eminently subjective area? The instruments so far available to psychosociology cannot verify the results of that kind of experiment by ruling out possible coincidences or simply the rational knowledge a person may have based on previous experience of the way the other individual reacts to a determined kind of stimulus."

"So why did you invent that collective of twin experts?"

"Gema, Isanusi is well-versed in psychosociology; as leader of the group, he needed to be. If I had openly told him about the limits of the theory of mental representation, I would never have been able to convince him it was possible to build those autonomous units. I needed a precedent, established by experts..."

"But the inadequacy of Sakharov's theory still exists. It might not be impossible that Isanusi manages to..."

Thondup cut in impatiently:

"You're getting carried away by what you'd like to believe, Gema. Without a solid theoretical basis, without properly controlled experiments, and without any means of verifying the results, it's practically impossible, and Isanusi knows it. That's why I invented those experts. Isanusi only knows the minimum about the study of twins, so he might believe me. Whereas if I'd said they were psychosociologists, he would immediately have found out the truth; he's up to date in that area, Gema."

"And obviously you had to tell him that the experiment had failed..."

"Because if it had succeeded, it would have been a real sensation; everyone would have known about it. That was obvious, Gema. Besides, it meant there was a plausible explanation for their failure: the need for each twin to assert their own identity."

"And yet the main point still stood: a group of specialists had devoted themselves to studying it, and therefore it was possible..."

"...in another group of people whose psychosocial characteristics were different," Thondup concluded.

Gema reflected on what she had heard and gave her agreement:

"There's no denying you did an excellent job given the circumstances, Thondup. But why didn't you tell me it was a fraud?"

"I thought about telling you, Gema, but I came to the conclusion it was better that you behaved sincerely, really believing it was possible. Otherwise, Isanusi would have become aware of the deception, and it would all have come crashing down. Tell me, knowing everything I've told you now, would you have behaved the same way all this time?"

She sighed:

"You're right." Her voice returned to normal. "What shall we do now? Isanusi might be affected by the fact that we can't establish an emotional contact, Thondup."

"I don't think so. There could be many explanations: your conditioning, physical exhaustion... Don't worry, I'll explain all that to Isanusi. I don't think you'd be able to deceive him."

"Thondup?"

"What is it?"

"What about the emotional flows I felt during my inductions?"

"Oh, that... Gema, how can you be sure they are real? You wanted to feel them, and it's only natural you did. Self-suggestion; that's the basis of my idea. And that is what will lead to Isanusi believing in the reality of his autonomous units. That will be enough to get him back to Earth, and there, attended by the best psychosociologists, it won't be long before he recuperates."

"I only hope so..." Gema looked at the time on the wall. "Thondup, it's time for your psychostabilizer."

"There's none left, Gema."

"None?"

"I used the last six hours ago." He added calmly, "Over the past three days I've been spreading out the time between doses; otherwise it would have run out twelve hours ago."

"And you haven't felt anything unusual?"

"Nothing. I hope my mind has stabilized."

Still slightly doubtful, Gema nodded:

"Yes, that is possible…"

Kay's elbow dug into Gema's ribs, and she whispered in her ear,

"Look at the little chicks…"

Without bothering to lower her voice, Gema replied,

"They'll soon grow wings, Kay."

Then she listened again to what Audo was saying:

"…return, we'll see each other again. I'll be waiting for you right here." He looked back at his new group. "With them: it's good for them to start getting used to the atmosphere in cosmodromes…"

The youngster had come to a halt beside Isanusi. Staring at the gleaming space shuttle, he asked,

"How high up is *Sviatagor's* orbit?"

"230 kilometers."

"Oh…"

Not knowing what else to say, the young man shuffled back to his group. Gema could not hold back a smile…

…And found herself back once more inside her pod. Speaking on the intercom, she said,

"Eidetic state concluded, Isanusi."

"So have I… Don't you feel anything now?"

Gema waited a prudent length of time before replying:

"No, nothing."

A sigh came over the intercom.

"Me neither… Shall we try again? For the last time today?"

"Alright."

"What episode shall we relive?"

"Let me think…" Gema's eyes fell by chance on the other pod. She informed Isanusi anxiously:

"Wait; something's wrong with Thondup." She called out to him: "What's the matter?"

He stopped struggling inside his pod. Raising his head, he looked across at Gema with some confusion.

"Oh, it's you…" He looked around the walls of the sick bay and asked, "What's happened to me?" He immediately corrected himself: "What's happened to us?"

"Don't you remember anything, Thondup?"

He frowned.

"I don't remember why I'm in here with you, in such a weakened state… What happened?"

Gema asked in a low voice,

"What shall I do, Isanusi?"

She listened closely and could just make out his whisper:

"*Ask him what he does remember.*"

"What do you remember about what's happened, Thondup?"

He rubbed his temples vigorously.

"We were approaching Titan, weren't we? We were ready to enter its orbit… I remember I lay down to rest a while. I wanted to be fully alert for when…"

His bewildered eyes alighted on Gema. "And when I woke up, here I am. What's happened?"

From the intercom came a further commentary:

"*Loss of memory, as a way of protecting mental stability…*" "Gema barely moved her lips:

"What shall I do?"

"*Explain to him everything that's happened; there's no reason to hide it from him.*"

Thondup was waiting, looking increasingly dubious. He inquired:

"What's wrong? Are you too ill to speak?"

Gema smiled at him.

"No, just a little fatigued, and wondering how best to tell you… Alright, listen, Thondup."

As Gema spoke, Thondup's lower lip began to droop. When she had finished, he murmured as if to himself,

"Almost unbelievable…" Then he spoke directly to Gema: "So everyone else is dead?"

"Not everyone; Isanusi is alive, remember."

"Yes, Isanusi…"

Staring blankly, Thondup bit his bottom lip. Then he fixed his gaze suspiciously on Gema and asked,

"Can I talk to him?"

"Of course; through the intercom. It's connected."

"Isanusi…" Thondup paused for a moment, staring pensively at the broken screen. "Isanusi, is there any error in Gema's explanation?"

"None, Thondup."

"Fine… Thanks." He looked across again at the other pod, blinking. "I'm sorry I didn't trust you, Gema, but…"

"I understand, Thondup. I can imagine the surprise you must have felt. I think you need to rest a while now." She indicated the control panel on Thondup's monitor. "Press the third button from the left on the back row."

He did so. A long needle appeared from the inner wall of the pod, then retracted almost at once. Thondup shivered from the unexpected jab but tried to keep a smile on his face.

"Perhaps when I wake, I'll have gotten my memory back." He blinked again. "In fact, if everything happened as you say, I'm not surprised I lost it." His words became slurred. He looked at Gema with troubled eyes: "A shame not to see Earth again…" His eyelids drooped and did not rise again. Gema spoke into the intercom:

"He's fallen asleep, Isanusi. How do I act around him in this state?"

The intercom took a long while to respond:

"It's difficult, Gema… It's obvious he has doubts, and he doesn't completely believe us. It's natural enough; his mind has tried hard to erase precisely those memories, and so he must resist them."

"Well then?"

"I don't know… We would have to create another story for him, one he could believe in. How could we explain what happened to the other crewmembers? I don't see a solution…"

"We could tell him the truth, Isanusi."

"Yes. That's the course we have to follow…"

"Gema! Gema!"

The voice roused her from her slumber.

"What is it, Isanusi?"

"I can see a ship on my radar."

Gema stiffened.

"Have you gotten in touch with them?"

"No reply. Maybe too far away; I'm trying to guage the distance."

"How do you know it's a spaceship?"

"It's changed course twice, so it can't be a comet…"

The intercom fell silent. "It's too far; it's in the planetary plane."

"Can't you steer towards it?"

"No. It's travelling away from the sun, in the opposite direction as *Sviatagor*. I would have to slow down, then accelerate again. I would lose it during the maneuver and wouldn't know where to head."

"Yes, I understand; it could change course again. Won't its radar pick us up as well?"

"Possibly... It could even be they're looking for us. But they won't be expecting to find us in this direction, Gema."

"What if we changed course two or three times...?"

"I'll give it a try."

A confused voice came from the other pod:

"Gema, what has happened?"

She replied in an urgent whisper:

"Isanusi has seen a spaceship. He's trying to establish contact."

"Another ship? What's it doing here?"

"It's probably looking for us, Thondup."

The sudden thrust of the engines pushed Gema's shoulder into the soft side of the pod. Thondup asked anxiously,

"What's that?"

"Isanusi changed course; perhaps that will make them realize this is *Sviatagor* and not a comet."

"Why don't we call them on the long-distance transmitter?"

"Have you forgotten? The directional antenna is broken, Thondup. You yourself checked it..."

Another thrust, this time in the opposite direction, so that Gema's shoulder lurched away from the pod wall.

"I don't understand... Can you please explain what another ship is doing in the neighborhood of Titan? Are they extraterrestrials?"

Gema stared at him.

"Don't you remember what I've already explained to you?"

"No… The last thing I can recall is that we were appro…" He broke off, waiting for the new thrust of the engines to finish: "… that we were approaching Titan, and I had gone to lie down so that I would be wide awake when we entered its orbit. Why are we here?"

He tried to get up from the pod but gave up. "I feel very weak, Gema. What's happened to us?"

Gema waved at him impatiently.

"I'll explain later." She spoke into the intercom: "Isanusi, have they shown any sign they have seen us?"

She waited a long minute for the reply. *Sviatagor* changed course a third time, and then the intercom spoke:

"I don't think so. They have changed course again, but not towards us. It's likely their radars aren't as powerful as ours…" The intercom fell silent for a moment. Then it announced:

"It's out of range, Gema."

She turned to face Thondup.

"Alright… I can explain what happened to us now."

Still staring up at the ceiling, Thondup asked,

"And did they succeed in finding life on Titan?"

"No."

"That's a shame. I remember that Pavel and Kay were very excited by that possibility. The number of dead worlds keeps growing, Gema."

"We can't say that for certain, Thondup."

He looked at her with surprise.

"Didn't you yourself tell me we didn't find life, Gema?"

"Life as we understand it on earth, Thondup; life based on carbon."

"Is there another sort?"

"There could be. It's true it hasn't been found yet, but the exobiologists refuse to rule it out."

"But if there had been another kind of life on Titan, we would have found it, Gema."

"It's not as easy as it seems, Thondup; in fact, if we don't know the specific characteristics of that life, it's very difficult. We need to start from the thermodynamic principle of life: a living being is a system that lessens its entropy by absorbing energy from its surroundings... but that is a principle that's too general to be of any use to us."

"But we spent six months there..."

"It would take years rather than months and a much more varied team than we had if we wanted to be able to dismiss the existence of another kind of life on Titan, or to prove it does exist. I'm surprised you don't remember anything about all this, Thondup: Kay always liked to talk about it."

Thondup said nothing and did not try to renew their conversation. Gema looked at him closely out of the corner of her eye. "He's thinking... What about? I'd really like to know."

Pointing an accusing finger at Gema, Thondup insisted in an exasperated voice, "Forget those fantasies, Alix; you're not Gema. She stayed on Titan with the others, on the temporary base we set up; or did you forget that as well?" He paused, still looking directly at her. Before she could answer, he went on: "And that collision with the meteorite never happened. It was the Titanoid who stowed away who made that hole in the nuclear reactor..."

He took a deep breath: "And above all, you're not going to die in five or six days... You aren't, and nor am I. The diagnostic machine," he waved an arm in the direction of the defunct equipment, "showed we were gravely affected, but not in any danger of dying immediately."

A low rumble reached the pod from the intercom:

"Has he fallen asleep, Gema?"

"Yes, Palas."

"There's no need to call me that if he's not listening…"

"Why did you go along with him? I almost believed I was the one who was mad, Isanusi."

"If I told him the truth he wouldn't have believed me either, Gema. His version is much nicer than the reality he's running from. You'll see, if you think about it: everyone alive ; a new form of life on Titan."

"Why on earth did I mention that possibility to him?"

"Don't worry; at least that version is inoffensive. He could have created something worse."

"Worse… But why does he have to change me into Alix?"

"Because she would have been the one they would have sent with him to tell people back on Earth. Besides, Gema and Kay would have had to stay on the base in order to study the Titanoids. See? His version is seamless, Gema."

"But I can't pretend I am Alix, Isanusi. There are a lot of personal things about her I don't know."

"That's not important. Thondup will put your lack of memory down to your physical enfeeblement, or to the shock at the appearance of the Titanoid and his destruction in the reactor."

Gema gave a lengthy sigh.

"Alright, I can see there's no other way… I'll have to be Alix."

"Like I am Palas."

"Isanusi, have you seen the spaceship again?"

"No."

"No doubt about it, we are nothing but bad luck."

"Don't exaggerate, Gema. What's really strange is that it came close enough for me to pick up its signal. Finding other ships is like finding the proverbial needle in a haystack. Gema, how about taking advantage of him being asleep to induct ourselves? Perhaps now we can make direct contact."

"Alright, let's try."

"...What I still can't understand is how the Titanoid got on board *Sviatagor*, when Kay and Gema had inspected the ship so carefully. Do you have any idea about that, Alix?"

"No."

In his pod, Thondup went back to his own thoughts.

Gema was slipping into her usual drowsy state when her companion shouted,

"I've got it!" He smiled at Gema triumphantly. "It was obvious; I don't know how they didn't see it..."

"What's that, Thondup?"

"The mineral samples, Alix."

"Do they have something to do with all this?"

"Yes..." Thondup's face darkened. "It's very serious," he concluded.

"Remember, Kay could not complete the study of their lifecycle."

"Not really..."

"We only saw adult specimens; we never found any examples of their other life stages."

"So?"

"In among the mineral samples we brought there must have been some embryonic forms, Alix."

"Latent, you mean."

"That's right. And that's what worries me: how can we be sure that there was only one latent Titanoid?"

"The samples are all different, Thondup. Besides, if there was another one, it would have appeared long ago..."

Thondup shook his head.

"No, Alix, I don't agree. Remember we know nothing about their lifecycle; other specimens could be in earlier stages."

He growled: "A fine situation we're in: heading for Earth with a cargo of exogenous forms of life."

"We can't be sure of that, Thondup. Perhaps there was only one Titanoid."

"Let's hope you're not mistaken, Alix."

Gema called out very softly,

"Isanusi?"

"Has he fallen asleep?"

"Yes, he has. I don't like the direction his hallucination is taking, Isanusi."

"Nor do I, Gema."

"What can we do?"

"Nothing." The intercom fell silent. "Gema, what's important is to reach Earth."

"I know."

"And to do that it's essential you two remain alive in my mind. Shall we try to induct ourselves again?"

"Go on then..."

"Look, look, it's there..."

"What is?"

"Another Titanoid."

"I can't see it..."

"Take a good look, now it's crawling along the wall."

"Thondup, the door is shut tight; it couldn't have got in here."

"*Look!*" There was a note of panic in Thondup's voice. Staring at a point on the wall, he murmured breathlessly,

"It's going through it."

"Through what?"

"The wall." He turned a face contorted by fear towards Gema. "Now things really are dangerous, Alix."

"Dangerous?"

"Don't you see? In its current phase it can pass through solid objects. How can we keep the Titanoids shut in?"

"It must be a transitory stage, Thondup."

"Possibly, but when they are in that stage they'll be able to escape from wherever they are being studied… Are you sure you didn't see it, Alix?"

"No, I didn't."

Thondup nodded pensively.

"I'm not surprised; they are much less well-defined than the other examples we saw on Titan… I could only tell where it was because of a slight change in the luminosity of where it was on the wall: tiny shadows and shiny dots appearing and disappearing… Yes, they're very hard to spot in this phase." He stared hard at Gema. "Alix, *Sviatagor* mustn't reach Earth."

"Why not? Those are the instructions Isanusi gave us; we can't disobey them, Thondup."

"If Isanusi knew what we had onboard, he would be the first to countermand them. We cannot take a strange form of life that cannot be isolated back to Earth. Remember, they are irrational beings; they will spread everywhere, causing irreparable damage in their quest for energy. And don't forget what that first Titanoid did when it crashed against the reactor."

"Thondup, when you say they are irrational, that's just a hypothesis, it hasn't been proved," Gema explained very clearly. "Even the case you gave of the other Titanoid could be interpreted completely differently: perhaps it was trying to examine the reactor. In any case, the new Titanoid has not crashed into it; it must have assimilated the first one's experience."

"That would be even worse, Alix. Don't forget that no irrational being has done as much harm to Earth as the rational being that inhabits it—mankind. If the Titanoids are rational, it seems obvious they must be primitive; they must have been aware of our presence, but have done nothing to establish contact of any kind. No, Alix…" His voice became firm. "*Sviatagor* must not reach Earth."

"Where then? The expendable fuel won't get us back to Titan."

"I don't know, Alix. Perhaps to Mars… That's it: Mars." He spoke a command into the intercom: "Palas, change course. We have a new destination: Mars."

The intercom did not respond.

"Didn't you hear what I said, Palas?"

"Wait, Thondup," Gema interrupted him quickly. "You've forgotten that I am the only one who can tell Palas to alter course."

"Do it then, Alix."

"I cannot go against…" She saw the look on Thondup's face. "Give me time to think, love; it's not so easy to plan a change of direction."

Thondup's face was tense, anxious.

"If this isn't just a delay tactic, alright then… Providing it doesn't take too much time. When will you have the new course set?"

"By tomorrow morning at the latest, Thondup."

"Alright."

"He's asleep at last, Isanusi."

"It took too long."

"He was very excited; he gets hysterical every time he sees a new Titanoid. It's really exhausting."

"I could hear you, you don't need to tell me."

"According to him, there must be at least ten of them on board. How are we going to deal with it, Isanusi?"

"I can't see any way. What you told him about the expendable fuel

I have left was correct; just enough to reach Earth and go into orbit around it. There's no chance of heading for anywhere else, let alone Mars; it's too far away."

"Couldn't you simulate a change of course?"

"How? He knows how long a trajectory change should take. And if I use up more fuel, the ship won't be able to reach Earth, Gema."

"What then?"

"Then you mustn't give in to him."

"Alright, I won't. But I'm sure he won't give way either."

"There's nothing I can do, Gema."

"That's true… Have you not seen the other ship again?"

"No."

Gema continued patiently:

"We've passed the critical point, Thondup. From our current position, and with the amount of fuel we have left, our only possible destination is Earth. If we aimed for anywhere else, we would not be able to reach it. Do you understand?"

He remained silent, his eyes fixed on her.

"Besides, remember that *Sviatagor* is not going to land but will stay in orbit, so there is no danger the Titanoids will reach Earth…"

"How can you be so sure? I can't, Alix. You have to understand that this is a form of life completely different from ours. Possibly its spores could reach Earth from orbit, and then what?" He moved his head slowly from side to side before going on: "You're the one who doesn't understand. We're talking about the Earth, about humanity. We must protect it at all cost."

Turning his back on Gema, he extended one leg outside the pod. Pushing with his arms, he sat swaying on the edge.

"What are you trying to do, Thondup?"

"I should have done it yesterday and not waited so long…"

Managing to shift his center of gravity outside the pod, he fell heavily into the polyfoam coating the floor of the sick bay.

"Thondup! Did you hurt yourself?"

Gema raised her head to try to see what had happened to him, but he was on the far side of the other pod. He did not reply.

"*Thondup!*"

Clinging to the side of her pod with both hands, Gema managed to rest her chin. Thondup's head appeared at the top of the other pod. He was crawling very slowly on his elbows, muttering to himself:

"*Sviatagor* mustn't reach anywhere inhabited by Man. We cannot allow those monsters to spread through the solar system..."

"Where are you going, Thondup?"

"... It's better for the two of us to die; Isanusi and the others will understand. Shame we had to leave the long-distance transmitter back at base; otherwise I could explain my motives to Earth and not let them think *Sviatagor* failed us..." He paused for a moment and patted the floor affectionately. "Yes, it's been a good ship; it's a shame they won't know that..."

Gema had managed to raise her shoulders level with the edge of the pod. Struggling to keep her head erect, she said,

"Please tell me where you're going, Thondup."

Thondup gave her a surprised look. He murmured,

"Alix... I was forgetting her." Addressing the face peering out of the other pod, he went on in a calm voice:

"No need to worry, my love; I'm going to do our duty."

"What duty are you talking about?"

"To stop the Titanoids reaching Earth... Goodbye, my love."

"And how do you plan to do that?"

Thondup had renewed his crawl towards the door.

"By removing the safety shield from the reactor."

"But it will explode!"

He nodded.

"And us along with it, I know… But the Titanoids as well."

"Don't go, Thondup; please, I beg you."

He halted and looked at her in genuine astonishment:

"Alix, I don't believe you. Are you suggesting we ignore our duty?"

"That duty doesn't exist! The Titanoids don't exist, Thondup!"

A hint of compassion appeared in Thondup's eyes.

"You're trying to escape reality again… Poor, poor Alix."

He resumed his crawling towards the door.

"Isanusi, what…?" Gema did not finish her question. "No, I mustn't put such a weight on him." She whispered urgently, "Farewell, my love," and switched off the intercom. "It's better for him not to hear." She measured the distance to the floor with her eyes: "Taking into account the layer of polyfoam, the reduced gravity and how little I weigh now…" She put her right hand on the bottom of the pod and tried to swing her left leg over the side. Her left foot reached the top, but only for an instant, before falling back… "Keep calm. Concentrate your energy." She looked inside herself. "Not enough."

She bit her lip.

"Perhaps I'll have sufficient strength if I distribute it properly. I have to be precise and quick and forget everything else… Let's try again." This time her heel hooked around the edge of the pod and did not slip back. "Keep going; there's no time to lose." She clenched the muscles of her body as tightly as she could…

Thondup pressed his cheek against the soft floor. He sighed:

"I'm so tired… as if I were two hundred years old, not twenty-two." He shook his head. "It doesn't matter. I have to get there, and I will." Setting his mouth in a firm line, he renewed his advance.

For an instant, Gema's body lay in precarious balance on the edge of the pod. "One last effort." She fell out of the pod, rolling over almost instinctively and pulling in her head. When she landed, the shock took her breath away. She gathered her strength. "Turn over." She turned onto her front. Still dazed by her fall, she looked around for Thondup. "There he is." Clawing her way across the polyfoam, she started out after Thondup. She could hear him indistinctly:

"...criticize you, Alix; I don't want to die either..." He drew breath. "I was with the group, with you, for so little time." Looking over his shoulder, a smile spread across his face and lips. "Are you coming to help me?"

"Perhaps there's still..." Gema begged him in a whisper: "Wait, Thondup, there's something important I have to explain to you..."

He glanced at her sadly.

"You'd better go back, Alix. You're not going to stop me."

Thondup fell silent and struggled to crawl more rapidly.

"No, there's no other way... Supposing he manages to stop now, what will happen afterwards?" She dried *the sweat? the tears?* clouding her eyes. "You made a mistake, Isanusi. You should never have brought the dead back to life... If you'd left me as I was, it wouldn't be so hard for me now..."

Thondup had reached the door. He pushed at it, but it was shut. Frowning, he muttered,

"I didn't remember..."

He looked up and saw the golden disc close to the doorframe.

"It's too high, I can't reach it with my hand."

He turned to lie on his back, with his right side against the wall. He calculated the trajectory his leg would have to follow:

"I can do it..."

He launched his foot upwards: the tip smacked against the wall close to the door contact. The pain in his toes made clench his jaw.

"It doesn't matter. Try again."

This time, his foot hit the disc, and the door slid open. Smiling, Thondup began to turn on to his front once again...

"I can't do any more." Gema halted, waiting for her breathing to return to normal. She tried to shake away the fog before her eyes, to see clearly... *"Nearly there... One final push, and..."*

Thondup's head was already out of the sick bay when Gema's hands grabbed his ankle and pulled him violently towards her. Caught by surprise, he wobbled on his elbows, and his head hit the doorframe. Gema saw the impact and how he collapsed. "Has he gone? I don't think he hit his head so hard... It must be a temporary loss of consciousness. I need to find out."

She dragged herself as quickly as she could up his inert body. "Luckily, I was right... If he'd been conscious, I couldn't have stopped him; he's managed to stay stronger than I have..." By now, her head was level with Thondup's. Holding her breath, she listened closely. Her forehead wrinkled. "He's still breathing; there's lots to do yet... But you can do it!" Raising her right knee, she placed it between Thondup's shoulder blades. Then she moved her left leg out to almost a right angle and braced her foot against the floor. She was just in time; Thondup was shifting feebly, trying to get her off his back and almost succeeding.

"Quickly, before he comes around completely." She thrust her right forearm forwards, trying to encircle his neck, but her weary muscles let her down, and it hung in front of Thondup's open mouth. Before she could position it as she had wanted, his teeth clamped down on her flesh. The pain galvanized her, and she wrenched her arm out of his mouth. Thondup opened his eyes and stared at the blood dripping to the floor. Horrified, he asked,

"Have I done you...?"

He was unable to say anything more: Gema's other arm had closed around his throat and was pressing on it, stifling his breathing. He writhed around, trying to escape. Gema could feel the energy draining out of her, fading fast: "I'm going to black out before I can finish ..." Calling on her last reserves of strength, she tensed all her muscles and pulled his head back, still pressing with her knee on his spine. Something cracked, and Thondup stopped moving. Gema collapsed on top of his lifeless body and burst into tears...

She slid slowly to the floor. She peered at the blood spurting from her arm and falling into the layer of polyfoam. "Best to end like this; there's nothing left for me to do." All at once she remembered and glanced over at the silent intercom. "I'm wrong; Isanusi needs to know there's no more danger." Her eyes searched for the pod in the sick bay, and finally found it. "It's too far away. I'll bleed to death before I reach it, I can't stop the hemorrhage..." Her face tensed: "I need to talk to him; to tell him that he can, that he *must* reach Earth, if only for my sake; all of this must not have been in vain..." She blinked confusedly: "What's this?"

The cloud approached, enfolding her in warm waves of affection? Compassion? Love?

"No, it's not real: all that nonsense about emotional telepathy is nothing more than a deception so that Isanusi can reach..."

The mist solidified into a steel-hard tentacle and pierced the armor plate that Gema had created to protect herself. Her mind was once more filled with a strange, pleasant sensation...

She still tried to resist. "No, no; Thondup explained it to me very clearly. There has to be a theoretical framework first and proper control methods; without those, it's almost impossible..." "Almost?" She lost the thread of her thoughts and struggled desperately to find them again.

"It's obvious, silly girl; it's just a hallucination. Because I want so, so much to feel Isanusi beside me now…"

Gentle colors filled her mental sky: From the distant horizon, countless memories flew towards her, surrounding her, penetrating her…

Gema was paralyzed with shock: "What's this? *They're not mine.*" She tried to escape, to fight her way back to the remote world outside. Her troubled gaze fell on Thondup's lifeless eyes. Scrambling quickly back into her interior world, other people's memories circled her again. Exhausted, she yielded, and they came flooding in. "Oh yes, now I know you were right, Thondup: it may only be an illusion… But why renounce it, when it's so beautiful?"

The curtain of mist trembled and evaporated; the figure of Isanusi rose before her. Gema ran to meet him, and they embraced tightly… He gently lifted her head for her to look. Gema saw them striding towards her: Pavel, Kay, Thondup, Alix… Their faces were calm. Happy.

A weak smile was just beginning to spread on Gema's lips as her heart stopped beating.

Epilogue

Because I always
Will happily fly
Whether I live
Or whether I die.

—E.L. Voynich, *The Horsefly*

A few weeks later

Little by little, the clouds ceased to be white; a thousand shades of red, violet and mauve replaced them, growing, mingling, until the sky seemed to be on fire… Then, very slowly, the colors lost their intensity, dissolving into a dark grey-blue: the sun had set.

Audo cleared his throat and felt for his pipe. As he began to fill it, shreds of tobacco fell into the grass without him realizing it: he was still gazing up at the evening sky. As he searched for his lighter, he cast an absent-minded glance around him. The trees were still visible, but the nighttime woods were closing in. Narrowing his eyes, the instructor peered through the gloom at the figure approaching him across the meadow. He was running and then walking, as if he could not catch his breath. It was too dark for Audo to distinguish his features.

"I'll have to wait until he gets nearer," thought Audo. He lit his pipe and carried on gazing at the line of the horizon where the sun had disappeared. "That's it for today; until tomorrow." He stood up, shaking off the flecks of tobacco on his clothes. Looking once more at the man approaching, the hand raising the pipe to his mouth halted in mid-air, and he stammered:

"Group 1-4 is currently finishing its sessions with the cyberpedagogues; I was just about to rejoin them..."

The member of the Cosmic Council nodded impatiently:

"I know, I know... But that's not why I came looking for you, Audo." He paused for a moment to get his breath back. The instructor waited, visibly perplexed. "You'd better come with me; I can explain everything on the way..." The Councilor took Audo by the arm and started walking back.

The man tapped on Audo's helmet and said,

"You can take it off; the air is breathable..."

Audo obeyed mechanically, as the man went on:

"The bodies have been removed, but until the atmosphere has been completely renewed, it won't be very pleasant in here."

Wrinkling his nose, Audo sniffed the faint smell of rot. He asked,

"How do I get to the bridge?"

The man pointed to the door:

"Through there."

Audo strode across the lab and opened to door. He called softly,

"Can I come in?"

A metallic voice answered from the control panel,

"Come in; I was expecting you."

The instructor blinked. "That tone of voice... No doubt about it, it's Isanusi." He went in, treading lightly.

The monitor spoke again:

"Sit down; you look tired."

"But how...? Of course, he can see me on the videophone."

Still staring at the empty screen, he went over to the captains' seat and sat down, murmuring,

"Thank you."

They fell silent for a long while. Finally, Audo made up his mind:

"I've been told everything that happened. I'm really sorry, Isanusi."

"The past is dead and gone."

"That's true. We need to concentrate on what we are going to do now. I was talking to some members of the Council before I came here; I think we can offer you a satisfactory solution to your... situation."

"I'm listening, Audo."

The instructor swallowed hard before continuing:

"We imagine that the loss of the rest of the group must be very painful for you..."

"You're not wrong. What about it?"

"We have psychoprofiles of all of them. These can be entered into the psychosimulator program, and it would be just the same as if they were alive: you could see them, talk to them..."

The monitor interrupted him:

"No, thank you. I never liked Dream Palaces."

Audo agreed, with a sigh.

"I told them I was convinced you wouldn't accept, but they insisted I mention that possibility first... it doesn't matter if you don't like the idea: we have another, rather more complicated one, that I think will satisfy you."

Something stirred in the cyberbrain's second memory system (or was it the fifth?). Isanusi said curtly,

"Go on, Audo."

"Several bodies are conserved in the Biological Bank..."

Isanusi and Gema exchanged a mental look. "Are you going to abandon us?" she asked. Isanusi did not reply. New clouds began to form in other parts of his cyberbrain... "You could be an instructor, or join another group. With your experience..."

"Another group?" wondered Thondup, in consternation, and his image trembled, became indistinct...

Alix said, "Leave it to him; he has to decide."

"Alright; let him decide alone," other voices responded, then the specters dissolved.

The echo reverberated around the walls of his skull: "Alone... alone... alone."

"Enough!"

Audo fell silent, staring in astonishment at the blank screen. Isanusi apologized in a softer tone:

"I'm sorry, Audo, but that solution doesn't satisfy me either."

"What would, then? I haven't been given any other suggestion for you, Isanusi..."

"I have one for all of you that is far simpler... Listen to me."

And Audo listened.

A few decades later

The pressure on her chest eased. Sarah took a deep breath. She wondered, "Is it over?" and looked up at the ceiling, where the numbers were displayed. "02-46-40; the acceleration has finished." Turning on her side in the bed, she peered at the body stretched out next to her. No sign of movement. "Lazy thing; he's fallen asleep."

She gazed at him, a smile on her face, for a long while… Then she stretched out and shook his shoulder, whispering,

"Wake up, Lars."

Immediately opening his eyes, the young man looked at Sarah.

"The acceleration has finished, lazybones."

"Just now?"

"No; a couple of minutes ago already."

Lars got up quickly and easily.

"Have they called us?"

"No."

He walked over to the videophone and pressed the control: the screen stayed blank.

"It looks as though it's broken down, Sarah."

"No, Lars, I disconnected the intercom."

Two pairs of eyes swiveled towards the doorway. On the threshold, Andrei gave them a friendly wink and said to the young man,

"Come with me; we need to check the engines."

Sarah wanted to know: "And what shall I do?"

"Wait for us in the relaxation room. Once we've finished we're having a meeting there."

The two men left the cabin. Sarah got up from her bed and looked at the door, puzzled. "A meeting? What for? It wasn't scheduled."

Aileen was chewing the end of her pencil hesitantly. She made up her mind, crossed out one word and wrote another alongside it. Sarah peered curiously over her shoulder at the sheet of paper covered in irregular lines and asked,

"Is it a new poem, Aileen?"

Aileen twisted her lips.

"If only…"

"Oh… don't be so modest, or we'll take away your title as the group's poet," said Wei, wagging a threatening finger.

Aileen protested:

"But I've never claimed to be that, Wei."

"So why do you write… that? I'm calling it 'that' because you say it's not a poem," Wei gave a theatrical sigh. "You women are so hard to understand! She writes them but doesn't write them. "

Inés leapt to Aileen's defense:

"Don't start attacking her, Wei. They may not be verses, but I like them. And I think that's good enough."

"No, it's not enough, Inés," Aileen contradicted her sadly. "When I read real poets and then look at what I do… I could cut my hands off; it's sacrilege."

"I don't think there's any need to go that far, Aileen. But I still don't understand; why do you keep on writing if that's how you feel?"

Aileen shrugged.

"I can't help it, Sarah. I look, listen, read… and feel. Then there's nothing for it: I have to express it, or I would burst. So I write and write until I've emptied myself… At that moment, it seems beautiful, but once the flame has gone out, when time goes by and I re-read what I've written, I feel like crying. There's nothing left, nothing…"

Karin patted her back in a friendly way.

"You're exaggerating, Aileen; they don't seem so bad to me… Why don't you read us this one?"

Sitting down on the couch, Wei said teasingly,

"Yes, read it to us now, while it's still good and hot! Ow!" He raised his hand to his ear, which Inés was twisting. "Alright, alright, I'll be quiet." She let go, and Wei rubbed his earlobe, protesting: "I should have asked for a spare pair of ears for this trip."

Karin smiled and asked,

"What's it called, Aileen?"

"It's called 'The Dream Palace.'"

Everyone in the relaxation room fell silent. Ida sat up on the couch she had been sprawled on, and Harold and Chaka raised their eyes from the chessboard to look at Aileen. Harold repeated the title, as if to himself:

"The Dream Palace…" In a louder voice, he said: "I don't care much for the topic."

"Be quiet; don't judge before you hear it." Karin turned back towards Aileen and encouraged her: "Start reciting it; don't pay him any attention."

"As you wish…" She stared down at the sheet of paper, then began to read out loud, in a slightly hoarse voice:

> I walk
> —alone—
>   Down the interminably long corridor.
> Hidden behind the glass, I can see their faces:
> They sleep and sleep, they dream…
> Dream that the Earth is theirs,
> Still.
> I might smile
>   Did I not feel
> The gaze of other eyes
> (countless eyes, wide-awake)
> Reading my thoughts… Yes, I walk alone;
> Alone among their dead.

Eyes shining, Harold repeated,

"…among their dead…"

He looked approvingly at Aileen: "Yes, those dead are calling out for vengeance, while we let their murderers dream."

Inés went up to him and stroked his tousled hair.

"The Federation has given its word, Harold."

"Their word? But on their side, they never kept their word, Inés."

"You have to understand that we cannot stoop to their level."

Harold raised his head, shaking it in disagreement.

"A condition like that should never have been accepted, Inés. It allowed them to escape the punishment they deserved."

Karin intervened in their dialogue:

"Without that condition, the Empire would never have dissolved, Harold, and we would still have that threat hanging over us. You yourself wouldn't be here. What does it cost us to let them dream? We have reality to explore, the entire Universe…" then she added, in a softer tone: "But we do understand you, Harold, we know you were born there…"

"Yes, it's always the same: you understand me, you understand me. But none of you have seen or heard…" With a weary gesture, he gave up: "There's no point discussing it any further." He searched for something in the front pocket of his spacesuit, but his hand came out empty. "Where can I have left it?"

"What's that?"

"My video-reader…" He frowned. "I remember; I left it on the captain's seat on the bridge." He got to his feet, and said, "I'll get it."

Karin took him by the shoulder. Annoyed, Harold turned to her.

"What do you want?"

"Nothing; I just wanted to remind you that Andrei told us we were not to go to the forward part of the ship until tomorrow."

"Oh that, Karin. Don't worry, I won't touch anything. I'll just pick up my video-reader and be straight back."

Seeing the pleading look in Inés' eyes, Karin took her hand away.

"Alright… Go and come back quickly: Lars and Andrei must be about to arrive."

Harold rushed out of the room. Inés smiled at Karin:

"Thanks; he really needed to get out of here… You know how he gets whenever the Empire is mentioned, or the Dream Palaces."

Karin's head drooped slightly. "I'm not sure I did the right thing, Inés: Andrei's order was clear…"

"Don't worry; I'll vouch for Harold: he won't touch anything."

At that moment Lars and Andrei came in through the door opposite the one Harold had left by. The group leader counted those present with a rapid glance and asked,

"Where is Harold, Karin?"

She looked across meaningfully at Inés, who flushed and replied,

"When you two didn't appear, he went to get his video-reader."

The group leader glanced at her, surprised.

"Where can he have got to? We checked all the cabins for stragglers on our way here but didn't spot him, Inés."

By now Inés' face had turned purple. She stammered: "He hadn't got left behind in his cabin, Andrei."

"Where is he then?"

"On the bridge."

Andrei turned to his second-in-command.

"Karin, didn't you tell him my instructions?"

"Yes, but…"

Inés came to her aid:

"I'm the one to blame, Andrei; Karin has nothing to do with it. If you wish, I'll go and look for Harold…"

The group leader sat down heavily on the couch.

"No, thank you; one is plenty. Besides, he'll be back at any moment."

Inés' face brightened:

"I'm sure he will, Andrei; he promised us..."

The other door to the room was flung open, and Harold entered almost at a run. When he saw them, he slowed to a normal pace.

Inés asked him, "Where's your video-reader, Harold?" Then, seeing how pale he looked, she paused and asked, "What happened?"

Harold dropped onto the couch next to Andrei. The others crowded around, curious to hear from him. The leader said calmly,

"Very well, Harold, you're back in time... I'm listening: what did you see?"

Moistening his lips, Harold cast a rapid glance at Andrei, then asked warily,

"Do you know?" Shaking his head, he answered himself: "No, that would be absurd; that is absurd."

Andrei insisted: "Tell us, Harold."

Harold stared hard at the group leader for, then nodded and began:

"Nothing happened until I reached the bridge. I saw the stupid video-reader exactly where I'd left it, on the captain's seat. I went over and bent forward to pick it up, but just as I was straightening up again, I saw the screen. That must have been when I dropped the video-reader a second time."

Karin impatiently ran a hand through her cropped hair.

"Harold, we're not interested in what happened to the video-reader; what did you see on the screen?"

"Well, I'm still not sure... I think, I'm almost sure it was a woman."

Karin cast him a puzzled look.

"No female crewmember has gone near the videophone, Harold."

He waved his hands dismissively.

"No, it wasn't any of you: if it had been, do you think I would have been frightened? It wasn't anyone I know, Karin."

"Why don't you describe her?"

"Long black hair, though not very much of it, and the face... the face was nothing more than skin and bone; I've never seen anything like it in all my life, I swear. Her skin was covered in small red blotches; her mouth was a thin line, her lips were barely visible. And her eyes..." He paused. "That was what truly frightened me: she was staring at me very seriously, as if she were asking me something... No, it was as if she could see right inside me."

He fell silent, his eyes fixed on the door he had just come through. Chaka pressed him:

"What did you do?"

"What could I do? I retreated backwards to the door, without taking my eyes off her. She didn't stop staring at me either... But she didn't do anything else. As soon as I had left the bridge, I shut the door as quickly as possible and leaned against it to recover. All of a sudden I heard a low laugh to my right..." Harold gazed apologetically at the others. "The first thing I thought was that it was all a joke one of you was playing; I turned swiftly towards the sound, and on the lab screen I saw another woman's face."

"It wasn't the same one?"

"No, this one had a normal appearance. She was even smiling; I thought she was mocking me. In fact, she wouldn't have shocked me at all, except that all I could see was her head... There was her smiling face, but all around her, the rest of the screen was blank."

Wei leaned back in his seat, annoyed:

"I think you're the one playing a joke on us, Harold. This is *Alice in Wonderland* and the Cheshire Cat, isn't it?"

The group leader calmed the offended Harold:

"Don't listen to him; I know you're not lying."

Harold glanced at him incredulously.

"How do you know?"

"I'll explain later; for now, you finish. What did you do when you saw the second face?"

Harold's cheeks burned.

"I came running back here..."

Andrei asked sympathetically,

"Can you describe her?"

"Not very well; I only saw her for a moment... She had short brown hair, with a reddish tinge to it..."

Andrei murmured: "No doubt about it; it was Kay."

"And who is Kay?" Aileen wanted to know.

The group leader waved away the question.

"We'll come to that, Aileen. I think we can start the meeting now..." When he saw their faces fall, he quickly added, "It's closely related to what happened to Harold; everything will be explained, you'll see." His voice returned to normal. "I must start by admitting I didn't like the idea of this trip either: a resupplying flight to Saturn, in an old-fashioned craft." He smiled: "Or, as Ida put it: 'the modern version of Noah's ark.'"

Ida raised her eyebrows.

"I have to say that I haven't changed my opinion, Andrei. Or rather, I have: now I think this is the Flying Dutchman's vessel. This is all we needed: ghosts on board. If I had known earlier, I'd never have set foot on *Sviatagor*."

"You'll understand, Ida; give me a chance," said Andrei, trying to mollify her. She shrugged, and he went on: "I didn't like the mission, but I accepted it. Someone has to take on the boring, unpleasant tasks... Now, however, I think differently: this isn't going to be an unpleasant trip."

"So what is it? An excursion through the solar system?"

"No, Wei: this is a new learning process."

"More learning? Didn't Ambar do her job properly? I can't think of a better instructor than her…"

"Calm down, Inés; I agree with you. This is about another kind of learning, if I understand correctly."

Karin spread her arms in bewilderment:

"Andrei: either my brain has lost the ability to understand, or you've lost the capacity to explain. What's all this about? And what does it have to do with what happened to Harold?"

The group leader sighed.

"How right you are, Karin. I think the best thing would be to start at the beginning. An hour before takeoff, one of the cosmodrome council came up…"

"Yes, I remember: it was Kim."

"You will also remember I was talking to him alone…"

"And when you came back, your expression had changed: you looked content."

"And I was, Aileen."

"Why don't you tell us what he told you?"

"I've been trying to do that for some time now and would have done so if you didn't interrupt me so often, Inés."

They all fell silent.

Andrei asked,

"Do any of you remember the Titan Expedition?"

They glanced at each other in embarrassed silence.

Only Lars responded steadily:

"It left in 2038. On the way back a year later, the entire crew perished in a collision with a meteorite; the cyberpilot succeeded in bringing the craft back to Earth."

A gleam of curiosity appeared in his eyes:

"If I'm not mistaken, the ship was called *Sviatagor*. It wouldn't be this one by any chance, would it?"

Andrei nodded, but before he could speak, Chaka protested:

"Just as I thought: we're onboard a museum piece, not an interplanetary craft. It can only travel at two hundred miserable kilometers a second..."

Andrei interjected:

"Yes, this is the same *Sviatagor*, Lars, but things didn't happen exactly as you said."

Ida gave a wry smile and ran her fingers through Lars' unruly hair. She murmured,

"Your fabulous memory is starting to fail you, my love."

Andrei wagged his finger at her.

"No, you're wrong, Ida. What Lars said is what is registered in the chrono-archives. Lars remembered correctly, but things didn't happen quite like that. The meteorite destroyed the cyberpilot."

"So who brought the ship back to Earth? Unless it was the ghosts that Harold saw..."

"You're almost right, Wei, but there's no need to look to another world. Three members of the expedition survived the crash, though badly wounded. They had no hope of making it back to Earth alive..."

"So what did they do, Andrei?" asked Karin, curious to know. "How did they manage to get back?"

"By connecting the cyberpilot up to the brain of the expedition leader... He is called Isanusi."

Inés shuddered.

"Are you trying to tell us... that he's still on board, Andrei?"

"Yes, he's still here, Inés. I hope you understand now why I disconnected the intercom at this end, and told you not to go up there." His eyes signaled the door to the bridge.

"Isanusi is asleep now, and he often has nightmares."

"So that's what I saw?"

"Yes, Harold."

Sinking further down into his seat, the youngster muttered,

"I hate this trip..."

At almost the same time, the rest of the group began to react:

"Why didn't they replace his brain in another body?"

"How come they let him carry on flying?"

"Why isn't this in the chrono-archives?"

"You say this is a learning flight. What can he teach us?"

"Can we trust him? He's an old man now, Andrei."

The group leader raised his hands calling for silence; little by little calm returned to the room.

"I asked myself many of the same questions, I can tell you. As you'll realize, Kim couldn't explain everything to me in an hour..."

His forehead was wrinkled in thought. "Although I'm not sure he really wanted to tell me everything. He had plenty of time to talk to me before then; he didn't have to leave it to the last minute. He led me to believe it would all become clear during our journey."

He looked up at them: "What I can tell you is why the story of the Titan Expedition is so little known: when *Sviatagor* returned, the Empire had just signed the Treaty of Adhesion, and all of Earth was focused on that..."

"But that doesn't justify the fact that the chrono-archives don't tell the truth, Andrei..."

"I don't know the reason either, Karin... But I can imagine exactly what would happen on Earth if all that got out: a lot of people would want to force Isanusi into another body and make him leave *Sviatagor*... I don't know why he prefers to stay here, but whatever the reason, I think we should respect his decision. But that's not the main point; there's something far more important, which Kim let me see."

"What's that?"

"All the groups who have gone on to become leading members of the Cosmic Council made their first flights in *Sviatagor*..."

Aileen shifted uncomfortably in her seat.

"Andrei, I must confess that being a leader... well yes, it is important, and yes, we need leaders... but I prefer exploration."

"We're agreed about that, Aileen. But one thing I forgot to say; the 'Tau Ceti' group also made their first flight in this Noah's Ark."

A fresh light appeared in the eyes of all those staring at their leader. Andrei went on, as if commenting casually:

"You remember that a new interstellar craft is being built..."

"Which is to travel to Altair..."

"And that as yet no crew has been assigned to it..."

"And it won't be ready for takeoff until after we return," Andrei concluded, with a smile.

All the group members exchanged delighted glances... all except Sarah. Frowning, Lars asked her:

"What's the matter? Don't you want to go to Altair?"

Her considerate eyes rested on him.

"Of course I do, Lars. But I feel so sorry for Isanusi..."

Her words brought a chill to the atmosphere. Bending forward in his seat, Harold murmured,

"I think Sarah is right; if my dreams were filled with images like that woman..." He shuddered. "I'd try never to fall asleep."

Andrei patted him on the back:

"But he does sleep, Harold." He looked around the group. "Isanusi asked me to tell you all that the first session begins tomorrow..."

Several millennia later

"...over and over again, the same journey; from Earth to Saturn, from Saturn to Earth. Until one day he didn't come back... (There is always a journey of no return.)

"But his story did not die with him. It has been transmitted through Time, has spread through space... You can travel the entire Galaxy, encountering other groups, and none will have forgotten his name, nor that on his journeys he received dozens of groups and returned them to Mother Earth transformed into Groups... Even if those are right who say that the story of the First Group is no more than a Legend (a legend as mystical as the fable of the Earth as the mother of mankind), Isanusi would not lose his meaning for us: he would not be forgotten. No, not even if that were true..."

— *Santa Clara, December 15, 1980 – October 21, 1981.*

About The Author and Translator

AGUSTÍN DE ROJAS (1949-2011) is the patron saint of Cuban science fiction. A professor of the history of theater at the Escuela de Instructores de Arte in Villa Clara, he authored a canonical trilogy of novels consisting of *Espiral* (*Spiral*, 1982), for which he was awarded the Premio David; *Una leyenda del futuro* (*A Legend of the Future*, 1985); a *El año 200* (*The Year 200*, 1990). The other two volumes in the trilogy are forthcoming in English translation from Restless Books. While he was heavily influenced by Ray Bradbury and translated Isaac Asimov into Spanish, de Rojas aligned himself with Soviet writers such as Ivan Yefremov and the brothers Arkady and Boris Strugatsky. After the fall of the Soviet Union, de Rojas stopped writing science fiction. He spent his final years persuaded—and persuading others—that Fidel Castro did not exist.

NICK CAISTOR is a British journalist, non-fiction author, and translator of Spanish and Portuguese literature. He has translated Cesar Aira, Paulo Coelho, Eduardo Mendoza, Juan Marsé, and Manuel Vázquez Montalban, and he has twice won the Valle-Inclán Prize for translation. He regularly contributes to Radio 4, the BBC World Service, the *Times Literary Supplement*, and the *Guardian*. He lives in Norwich, England.

CUBAN SCIENCE FICTION FROM RESTLESS BOOKS

MIGUEL COLLAZO
The Journey

ORLANDO LUIS PARDO LAZO
Abandoned Havana

AGUSTÍN DE ROJAS
A Legend of the Future
Spiral
Year 200

YOSS
A Planet for Rent
Super Extra Grande